MAXUM & LILY

REBEL GUARDIANS NEXT GENERATION

LIBERTY PARKER

DARLENE TALLMAN

CONTENTS

	Acknowledgments	viii
	Blurb	ix
	Prologue	1
1.	Lily	7
2.	Lily	19
3.	Lily	29
4.	Maxum	38
5.	Lily	48
6.	Maxum	57
7.	Maxum	67
8.	Maxum	84
9.	Maxum	95
10.	Maxum	109
11.	Lily	120
12.	Lily	131
13.	Maxum	139
14.	Lily	149
15.	Lily	159
16.	Maxum	167
17.	Maxum	177
18.	Lily	184
19.	Maxum	194
20.	Maxum	203
21.	Maxum	217
22.	Maxum	230
23.	Lily	239
	Epilogue	249

Liberty Parker's Follow Links:	256
Darlene Tallman's Follow Links:	258
Also by Liberty Parker	260
Also by Darlene Tallman	263

COPYRIGHT

Maxum & Lily
Rebel Guardians Next Generation
Book 3

Published by Liberty Parker & Darlene Tallman
Cover by: Dark Water Covers
https://goo.gl/mhVY1Y
Model: Will T.
Photographer: @Paul Henry Serres Photography
Edited by: Mary Kern, Joanne Dearman, Kat Beecham, Melanie Gray, Shannon McFadden, Beth DiLoreto
Proofread by: Charmane Brooks
Formatting by: Liberty Parker

authorlibertyparker@yahoo.com
ddean228@yahoo.com

MAXUM & LILY

LIBERTY PARKER
DARLENE TALLMAN

DEDICATION

These never get easier to write, simply because there are so many people in our lives that mean so very much. However, this time, it's for anyone who has ever traveled a broken road to get them to where they ultimately belonged.

ACKNOWLEDGMENTS

We can't do this gig without some pretty important people in our lives – our PAs, Nicole Lloyd and Sharon Renee – who keep us on the straight and narrow. Well, mostly, that is! We also couldn't do it without our 'girls' – Melanie, Kat, Beth, Shannon, Joanne, and Mary – who make sure our words are the best they can be. Lastly, our awesome cover designer and sweet friend – Tracie Douglas – who covers our words so beautifully. We love y'all to the moon and back, ladies!

BLURB

Growing up in the shadows of everyone in the Rebel Guardians, Lily finds that it's hard to break free of the 'little girl' mentality that her parents, as well as her aunts and uncles, have, at least where she's concerned. Maybe it's because of the issues she's had since she was a teenager, but living under the proverbial thumb has gotten on her last nerve. Toss in a biker who has commitment issues, and she's all over the place emotionally. When her brother, Luca, asks her to come visit, she practically tosses everything into her car and takes off.

The first time he saw her, she was just a little girl. Even then her soul called to his, he watched her bloom into a beautiful, courageous woman. Maxum feels cold and dead inside… unless she's around. As she's grown and matured, his thoughts for her have changed from that of a brotherly type of love. She's no longer a gangly little girl, she's a siren, a vixen, a charmer and he's under her spell. But his past won't allow him to love her, to honor her, to give her everything her heart is all but begging him for. But things come to light, and Maxum must make a decision. It'll be the hardest one of his life. Time to face those demons and overcome the monsters that sleep under his bed.

When the past threatens the future, who will remain standing?

Suitable for ages 18+ due to language and adult situations

PROLOGUE

Lily (Age 12)

"Nan." I dizzily make my way into the nurse's office. "My head, it hurts really bad." My hazy vision is making it near impossible to walk straight without running into the walls. Nan is volunteering in the nurse's station this week. I am always happy when she works in our school. She started off as a nurse and worked her way up the ladder to receive her degree in teaching.

"Lily, dear." She rushes her way over to where I'm slumped against the door. Grabbing me up in her arms, she slowly escorts me over to the cot. Gently, she lowers me down and my eyes close, the light is so bright that my head begins pounding, hurting, making me feel sick to my stomach. "Tell me what all you're feeling." She begins rubbing her hand over my face, making me feel safe like she always has the ability to do.

"My head, Nan. It hurts," I begin to explain.

"Is it all the time, or does it come and go?" she questions.

"It comes and goes… but lately, it's happening more and more." My tongue feels heavy and my eyes are burning. It hurts to talk, to concentrate for longer than a minute at a time, and all of her questions are making my world spin on its axis.

"So, it's frequently happening... like every day? Every other, twice a week? Give me more details, Lily Bug."

"Every day, a couple of times a day. It's getting harder to get up and move. I just want to sleep. Can I go home, Nan? I'm so sleepy," I all but beg her.

"Let's put a cloth over your head and rest your eyes for a

bit. It may help, I would prefer you to be here with me for a while, if things don't change in an hour, I'll call your mom and dad… deal?"

"Sure, Nan," I acquiesce. I'd prefer to be home in my big, comfy bed, but if Nan wants me here, here's where I'll stay. Dad and Mom won't go against her judgment, and I'd hate calling them from work if this eases up soon.

"I'm gonna dim the lights for you, get some rest and we'll see what happens when you wake up."

"Yes, ma'am," I respond, drifting off to sleep.

"Lily, it's time to wake up now, the school day is almost over. You need to get back to class and gather up your belongings." Nan lightly shakes me awake.

My eyes shoot open and my hand clamps over my mouth. "Gonna be sick," I say, right before fluids spew from my body. As soon as I stop heaving, I look around and see that the nurse's station now resembles a scene from that movie *The Exorcist* that my parents watched with us kids last weekend. I still shiver when I think of how that girl's head spun around. "I'm sorry, Nan." I apologize for giving her more work to do before heading home.

"Don't you worry your pretty little head, Lily Bug. I love you, now go get your things together while I clean up. We'll be heading over to see Dr. Bowerman before taking you home."

My shoulders slump. "I don't wanna go see him, Nan. He always finds some sort of shot to give me when I go in."

"You're overexaggerating, girl. Now shoo." She points to the door. I do as requested… but make sure my displeasure is known as I kick my feet and mutter under my breath.

"Sass, girl, watch your mouth!"

"Yes, Nan!" I holler back as I walk down the hallway toward the class I was excused from to get my backpack. I was *too* sick to remember to grab it as I hauled butt out of the door. As I make my way closer to the room, the world starts spinning around me and I drop to the floor. My hands come up to hold the sides of my head when I hear Luca shout my name.

Then, nothing. It's silent as the blackness pulls me under.

Maxum (Age 16)

"You're nothing but a fucking whore!" Dad screams at Mom. I can hear their fight from my bedroom and even though I'm supposed to 'be a man' according to my dad, I feel my entire being shaking from fear. I've grown up in hell; my parents argue constantly and it usually degenerates into him calling her vicious names and making her cry. I don't understand why she doesn't just leave. Why *we* don't leave. Because he sure as hell acts as if we're both a bother to him. Hell, she doesn't know that he's smacked me around whenever she's not home. He's been careful not to leave bruises where others can see, and the few broken bones were explained away as me doing something 'stupid' when the doctor asked. Once again, I pray that this time, she leaves and takes me with her.

I close my math book. There's no way I can focus on homework when it sounds as though World War III is going on in the living room. Standing, I take a deep breath and head into the fray to see if I can get him to focus on me and leave her alone.

"Dad?" I ask when I reach the living room. I don't see Mom anywhere and didn't hear her crying when I passed their room. "Where's Mom?"

"Gone." He's blunt and to the point and won't look me straight in the eyes.

"To the store?" It's not her usual day to go grocery shopping, but maybe she forgot something.

"No, you idiot. She's gone for good. It's just us from now on, boy." Fear of it being just us engulfs me, but I've learned not to let it show. I've only got two years until I'm old enough to be on my own, so hopefully, I can survive.

"Uh, okay." My brain is swirling and I wonder why she didn't take me. I don't dare ask him, though. I can still see the anger radiating from him and don't want it directed at me.

"You need to remember this, Maxum. Women are only good for *one* thing, getting your dick wet. Relationships are useless."

I nod before I head into the kitchen for something to drink. Based on their stellar example, I will never allow my heart to get involved with anyone.

1

LILY

Dr. Bowerman has been seeing me since I was in diapers. He went from my pediatrician, to my physician. I was diagnosed with hormone headaches when I was twelve. My hormone levels are low, some dangerously so and some non-existent. Today is my first Bio-TE treatment, and my hopes are high that these pellets being inserted into my hip, will work better than the cream I was applying daily to my wrist. The cream stopped working as well as it did when I first started using it, and this small surgical procedure is supposed to be the best solution for my 'issue'. I sure hope so because the headaches are debilitating and when you add in the period from hell, I usually lose a week of my life once a month. Of course, I have breakthrough headaches, but they can generally be handled with the medicine Dr. Bowerman prescribed. Still, growing up with this has been difficult for not only me, but also my family.

I still remember that very first one, when I passed out in front of Luca. As soon as I woke up in the emergency room, I saw my dad and mom. The look of anguish on my dad's face gutted me. He may be a badass biker, but that day, I saw the fear of the unknown on him and his tears flowed freely. Luca was in the bed beside me rubbing my head and holding my hand. He's been one of my best friends since we were kids and even now, he checks in regularly. In fact, he's the one who researched my headaches and found out about the Bio-TE. If it works, I may owe him a cake or something. I just want to live a normal life, not one that is based around my damn period!

"Are you ready for this, young lady?" Dr. Bowerman inquires as he comes into the room with his nurse, Rebecca.

"Since I don't know what to expect, I don't know how to answer you," I reply.

"It's an easy procedure, we will give you a numbing shot to deaden the area on your hip. Once you're good and numb, I'll use a scalpel and cut a long enough incision to pop the pellets in. It won't be deep, but I do need to press them in, so it may end up feeling uncomfortable. Do you have any questions?" he asks me as Rebecca brings him a needle and a vial full and ready. "You'll need to lower your pants as far as you can. I need to be able to reach your side between your cheek and waist." I blush when I realize I'm wearing my comfy panties. They are old, ugly and stained. How embarrassing that a man that's been taking care of me since I was a child will see how ill-prepared I am. "Are you okay, Lily?"

"Hmm? Sorry, I spaced out."

"You just got a little red in the cheeks. Are you feeling well today?" His look of concern is touching, but I'm not sick, I'm embarrassed.

"I-I'm fine," I stammer as I do what he's asked. Rebecca smiles at me and I realize that she knows why I'm so flustered. She pats my shoulder to try and comfort me, but I've already made a mental note to hit the store and buy new underwear.

The procedure is over before I know it and I'm soon getting myself straight. "Now, it can take up to three treatments before we start seeing results," Dr. Bowerman cautions. "They're done three months apart, so we'll get your appointments set up. Do you have sufficient refills on your breakthrough medication or do I need to send over a prescription?" he asks.

I stop to think about what I have at the house. "I can't remember so maybe you should send it?"

"I know you won't overuse it, so that's what I'll do. Remember, if it doesn't work, go to the hospital and they'll give you an IV cocktail of medicines."

I nod because I'm very familiar with our local emergency room. I think we should own a wing by now. The Rebel Guardians aren't a one-percent club, but the businesses they do have, has yielded plenty of mishaps over the years. "Thanks, Dr. Bowerman," I say.

"You're welcome, Lily. I'm glad Luca found this stuff. Granted, I had to get certified to use it, but I didn't mind. It might be a game changer not only for you, but for several of my patients who have similar issues."

I can't help but smile when he says Luca's name. Ever since he moved in next door to me, before our parents got together, he's been my protector. I know that growing up, friends were sure we were more than friends, but that's simply not the case. Me, Tig, Luca, and Ralynn were thicker than thieves and there was never anything romantic between any of us. "That's Luca for you. He's always watched out for me, even when we were kids."

"He's a good man," Rebecca says. "All of you kids have grown up to be responsible, hardworking adults. I'm sure your parents are proud."

"They are, but we had wonderful examples growing up, Rebecca," I tell her as I gather my purse.

"Oh, one more thing, Lily," Dr. Bowerman says. "You can shower, but you can't submerge yourself for forty-eight to seventy-two hours. The patch can get wet, but it can't get soaked."

"Okay, so no Saturday night baths. At least the twins' birthday party isn't for a few weeks because they're having it at the water park and there's no way I can resist those slides."

He nods at me. "You should be good by then."

"Alright, anything else I need to be aware of?" I can't think of anything because we did a thorough research of this product, but you never know what the doctor will come up with.

"No. If you have any issues, any problems arise, or you just have a question, don't hesitate to call the office." He reaches over and gently squeezes my shoulder. "You're going to be fine, Lily," he reassures me as he grabs my chart and swiftly follows Rebecca out the door.

"Well…" I say to myself, "that was fun." I didn't allow anyone to come with me, wanting to do this on my own, but now, I'm regretting that I have no one to ride home with.

Maxum

I'M UNDERNEATH THIS FUCKER'S HOTROD, TRYING TO mentally piece together what this motherfucker was doing when he ran off the road and into a ravine. There's nothing wrong mechanically that would've caused this, but he's a dumb fuck teenager with a lead foot. Nothing would surprise me.

"Maxum, you almost done caressing that car?" Jaxson asks me.

"Nah, man, a car like this deserves TLC… not that the owner gives two fucks," I respond. "I'm happy the brothers supported me with opening up this shop, but sometimes I feel like I'm in over my damn head." A frustrated sigh leaves me when I inform him of this.

"We got you, brother. You just gotta speak up so we can shift some people around if we need to. Most of the other businesses have townspeople working the shifts, so we could bring in a few of the guys who have automotive experience." The fact that he is trying to help me problem solve my backup issues, reminds me once again what the brotherhood means to me… to both of us.

"Might not be a bad idea. I want it to grow since there's nothing nearby. If we get too backed up, we won't be able to expand the way I think we can." My thoughts have been going nonstop trying to figure out ways for the company to grow and expand. I didn't want to bother the brothers with any of this, since they went out of their way to financially and emotionally support me.

"What if we see if we can get a few of the brothers to be dedicated to the bullshit stuff? You know, oil changes, tire rotations, state inspections. That kind of thing. It would free us up to do the body work and major repairs," he states.

"I like that idea. Hell, if any of the women can do it, we can bring them on as well. Equal opportunity and all that shit." I would trust a sister before I would an outsider, and now my thoughts are stuck on which one I can talk into coming and helping me out.

"You're just hopeful that Lily would want to be here so you can spend more time with her," Jaxson teases.

"Naw, it's not like that with us. I'm not in the market for a long-term relationship, and she's the kind of woman who needs red roses, romance, white picket fences and shit," I reply. Although if I were built like that, I'd definitely choose Lily. Our time in the cabin was unbelievable, but I knew even then that I couldn't let it go further. She deserves the world and I can't give her that, thanks to my upbringing. My father did his best to show me that women were nothing more than mere objects to be used and abused. I don't want to be that man; I'd rather be alone in life than make another person miserable.

"I think you're wrong, brother," Jaxson says. "But if you're not serious about a relationship with her, you need to cut her loose. Axe won't like it that his little girl is being played with, especially not by a brother." Does he think I don't know all of this? I'm very aware, which is why I've made sure she knows we go no further than a roll in the sheets every once in a while. I like her, value her friendship, and I can't lose her. She knows she only has to say the words and we'll stop what we've been doing. Or did… fuck, I don't know if we're still doing the benefit thing or not. It's been a few weeks since we burned up the sheets; at night when I'm lying in bed all alone, I miss her presence, warmth and laughter.

I nod even though I'm still under the car and he can't see me. I've kind of been waiting for Axe to pull me aside and question me about my intentions toward his daughter. She's the 'original' club princess and acts like it through and through, but my dad's words supersede anything I might actually want.

"Brother, you know that what you experienced growing up is not the norm," Jaxson states. He knows more than most since he's my best friend, but he still has no clue that for sixteen years, I was witness to the emotional and sometimes physical abuse my father heaped on my mother. Then, for two years before I split at eighteen, he spewed his poison about women and relationships. Granted, since becoming a member of the Rebel Guardians, I've seen how relationships *should* be, what with pretty much every older brother finding and claiming his old lady. But that's not for me.

"Hard habit to break, Jax," I say. "You hear how women are only good for one thing twenty-four seven and tell me how it fucks with your mindset."

"Jesus fucking Christ, Maxum. You see how all the brothers are with their old ladies, right? You think that's an act or something? I can tell you, it's not and if you examine your heart, you'd know I'm telling the damn truth. Each one of us would lay our own lives down for our women. Hell, we'd lay them down for our brothers' women as well."

"Look, I know you're all in love with Ralynn and shit, but that doesn't mean that we're all gonna find and settle down with our one true love. I'm not trying to be an asshole, but don't try and force me to live a lovey-dovey type of life-style… it's just not in the cards. Not for me and Lily, not for me and anyone. I'm meant to be alone, and that's the way it is and is always gonna be. I won't tie anyone down with the fucked-up mess that repeats in my head daily… it's not fair to a woman and children stuck with my fucked-up ass."

"Then you need to cut her loose, brother. She doesn't deserve to be strung along like you're doing if there's no future," he says. I can hear the censure in his voice and sigh. I don't want to be at odds with my best friend and if I don't give Lily up, it's going to cause us problems. I don't know that I can let her go, though.

"We have an understanding, Jax. She knows all she's gotta do is say stop and we quit. I've never hid what I do and don't want from her, she's a big girl and can make her own damn decisions. Let it go and keep your nose clean of me and Lily and whatever sort of relationship we're having. We're both happy and content for now. When that changes, we'll move on."

"You're an asshole, Maxum. That girl is in love with you and has been for a long time now. She'd say anything just to be even a small part of your life and it's time you woke up and realized that!" Jaxson shouts.

"Are you on your period or something, Jax? Are we gonna paint each other's toes and give facials? Do I need to set some time aside for girl talk? Stop being a pansy and look down. Last I checked you had a dick not a fucking pussy." My irritation at his interference is pissing me the fuck off!

"I can't with you today! This is all gonna blow up in your face and when it does, don't say I didn't warn you. I'm out," Jaxson growls out as he stomps away.

"Well, that went well," I mutter to myself. "The conversation started out on a good note, then he had to go and bury his nose where it doesn't belong."

"Talking to yourself again?" I hear the voice of an angel and slide out from under the car so I can see her face. Just because I can't commit to her, doesn't mean I don't want to see her beautiful face and hear her angelic voice every chance I get. I need it buried deep in my soul so that when she gets tired of me and moves on, I have something to hold on tight to. These times with her will get me through my miserable existence.

"Well, you know, I like myself better than most other people. At least with myself I know I'll have a great conversation," I jokingly state. God damn, she's fucking beautiful!

2

LILY

I start laughing at his words. It's one of the things I love about him, his sense of humor. Before I can reply, he asks, "How was your appointment?"

"It went pretty well. Got the injection of Bio-TE so we'll see if it helps with the headaches or not," I reply. My 'condition' is well-known in the club as many of them have had to haul me to the emergency room for the cocktail, Maxum included.

"I hope so, babe," he says. "Hate it when you're in pain like that."

"Yeah, you probably hate the puking as well," I joke. He's held my hair back plenty of times as I've puked my guts out. I don't even get embarrassed any more since it's happened so often.

"Don't much care for you looking like death warmed over," he replies. "So, if this shit that Luca researched helps you, I'm fucking thrilled."

I look up at him; he's everything I've ever wanted in a man, but he told me early on that he wasn't relationship material. I keep holding out hope that he'll see that we're different and decide to go for it, but I don't know how to approach that topic. Instead, I'll let it go for now and take what he's willing to give me for now. "You want to come over later?" I ask. It's been a few weeks since we've spent any time together and I have to admit, I've missed him. Of course, he hasn't reached out to me, so maybe he's tired of our relationship.

"Not sure, babe. I'm backed up right now and then have to do the paperwork before I can't catch up."

"You have paperwork that needs doing? Jesus, Maxum,

why didn't you say something? I know how to do that shit with my eyes closed. What do you think I do for the club's businesses? Hell, you probably don't even have a website, do you?" The look he gives me would be comical if it wasn't so important to the growth of his garage. He looks as if he's constipated as he contemplates my words. I imagine the light bulb going off in his head before his head whips over in my direction. I watch his eyes widen at my words.

"You can help me with that? You're hired!" He pulls me into a hug and I breathe in his scent. Motor oil, leather, and the bodywash he uses that has a crisp, clean smell. It feels like home in his arms, although I'll keep that to myself. "Do you have to work here? How will that play out?"

"Once I get everything straightened out in your office and set up your website, I can work pretty much anywhere as long as I have my laptop and Wi-Fi," I reply.

"So, you'd what? Be like a satellite employee? How will we ever stay on top of that damn stack of daily paperwork if you're not here?" I wanna laugh at the worry sketched across his face. He really has no idea what all I'm capable of doing, and he knows me intimately… it's sad and pathetic if you stop and think about it. He knows what my skin tastes like, what noises I make when I come, and yet, he knows nothing about what I do for a living. I'm saying where we're concerned, we're batting zero. I pay attention when he talks to me, while he's the typical male; he hears what he wants and the rest he just makes the fuck up.

"Maxum, I can work from here and satellite into the other websites once I get the paperwork that you've got taken care of," I state.

"Fuck, this might save my ass," he mutters.

"That's what I'm here for. To keep that lush ass full, can't have it wearing down… it looks too damn good in a pair of Levi's." I snort out laughter at my own words.

The look he gives me is full of desire and he grabs my hand and pulls me close. "C'mon, let me show you what you're working with, babe," he whispers. "Then I think we're done for the day, unless you've got something else to do."

"I-I'm supposed to run by and see my mom." I can't blow her off, either. I've done that several days in a row and got the 'stern-voiced' Mom when she called and left a voice-mail about today. If I miss it, then I'll have to deal with my dad and when Mom is upset, he pulls out his president voice. I try to avoid that as much as possible.

"How about you go see your mom and I'll wait for you to text me. I'll order Chinese for delivery and you can just come here instead." He has great boyfriend potential; I just wish he'd recognize these traits in himself the way that I do.

"Yeah, that'll work. Do you want me to write down what I want?" I hold my breath because I may know a lot of his likes and dislikes, but I don't think he pays attention to mine. It's crazy to worry over if he knows what foods I like and which ones I dislike when just a second ago the worst I was concerned with was that he has no clue what I do for a living… for the club, his club.

He scoffs. "Are you kidding? You either want beef pepper steak with fried rice, or pepper chicken with green beans and fried rice. Do you know which you're in the mood for tonight?" he asks. I'm so shocked that he knows what I want that I'm speechless. When I don't answer, he says, "I'll just get both, with plenty of that duck sauce you like, and eat whichever you don't." Color me surprised; I'm surprised my eyes aren't popping out of my head with the knowledge that he does know something about me that I personally consider important. I'd cut a bitch if she tried to mess with my Chinese food… okay, so I'm a little obsessed. I have stabbed Ralynn with my fork before when she tried to take some chicken from my platter. I love her, but I don't love anyone that much.

I'm not a good sharer.

Never have been, just ask my parents if you don't believe me.

That's in *all* aspects of my life.

"That sounds good to me, Maxum. Now, show me the paperwork pile from Hell," I tease, as I bump my shoulder against his then I end up taking his hand. I try to be affectionate without being pushy and sometimes, he goes along with it, like right now. He laces our fingers together and drops a kiss on my forehead before walking beside me to his office. When I see the desk, I groan because it's going to take a few days to get it organized before I can actually work. "Guess I know what I'll be doing the rest of this week," I state, looking around. Wow, he wasn't joking when he said he was behind.

He rubs his neck and grins. "Sorry, babe. But it's not my fault; I had no clue I'd be slammed every day when I opened the place."

"We'll get you on track, Maxum," I promise. "I'll get started tomorrow."

Maxum

I FINISH MY DAY, THEN HEAD UPSTAIRS TO MY SMALL apartment over the garage to take a shower and get cleaned up. Once done, I order our Chinese for delivery then settle in to watch a ball game. My thoughts are all over the place from my earlier conversation with Jaxson, as well as briefly seeing Lily. "Fuck you, Dad," I grind out. "If you hadn't fucked my head up, I would claim her in a heartbeat. But no, you were a Grade-A asshole and that has colored every 'relationship' I've ever been involved in." If he hadn't taken off, I'd probably go beat the shit out of him.

Thoughts of him swirling, I get up when I hear a knock on the door. Expecting the delivery man, I step back when I come face to face with my president, Axe. "Pres?" I question.

"Thinking it's time we have a talk. Don't you?" he asks as he pushes his way into my apartment.

"Um… sure," I draw out. Not one-hundred percent sure what he's doing here, but I have a good idea of what talk we need to be having. "Would you like a beer or something?" I walk to the fridge and pull one out, not sure if he wants one, but I'm suddenly parched.

"I'll take a beer, brother." Well, he's not acting like he plans on rearranging my face and knocking out a few teeth. "Go ahead and have a seat and I'll bring it to you." I take a deep breath before turning my back on the one man who has the power to bring my life crashing down around me. "Bottle or can?" I ask, trying to prolonging the upcoming conversation.

"Either works," he dryly responds. He knows what I'm doing, and I'm grateful he's giving me this play. I need time to wrap my head around the fact that Axe is here, surely to confront me. I know that the entire MC is aware of mine and Lily's relationship status, but since it's nothing more than a friends with benefits sort of thing, I never asked Axe for permission to romp around in the sack with his daughter. As far as he needs to know, we're just friends… he doesn't need to know how good of friends we actually are.

"So, what can I do for you, Axe?" I ask as I hand him his beer.

"I'm gonna get right to the point. What's up with you and my girl?" I take a swallow of my beer to chase the god-awful taste away. This isn't something I ever wanted to sit and converse with him on.

"We're friends, Axe. Nothing more, nothing less." I emphasize the word nothing each time it leaves my mouth. "Why?" I wanna know where his thoughts are taking him.

"We both know for her, it's more than friendship,

Maxum." He sighs while running his fingers through his long beard.

"It's not," I implore. I don't feel like eating my teeth, I like my smile the way it is.

"Maxum. Don't play coy with me, boy. I may be old, but I wasn't born yesterday." I can tell by his tone that he's getting a bit perturbed with my innocent act.

"Axe, I don't know what you think it is, but we're simply friends," I insist again.

"Maxum, I know my daughter. I also know that she sees the pot at the end of the rainbow with you. She's thinking of y'alls future, so if you can't give that to her, you need to step back." Fuck, now he's using his president voice. I hate when he does that because I feel like a little kid again, getting scolded for doing something wrong.

"We have an understanding, Axe. We're good together, but I'm not ready for anything permanent." I don't share my feelings well; this is the best he's gonna get out of me.

"I'm gonna ask you to stop seeing her. Not as your president, but as her father. She deserves so much more than you're willing to offer her. Think of her, not your hormones, Maxum. She's the best thing that's ever happened to me and the second I held her in my arms, I vowed to protect her from anything and anyone who could harm her in any way."

Fucking hell. He's serious and I'm not sure that I can give her up. "Axe, you're overstepping here. We're both consenting adults, not teenagers." I may be taking my life in my hands, but what Lily and I have or don't have is none of anyone's fucking business. I'm tired of their bullshit and this is the last straw.

"Maxum, I won't allow you to break my daughter's heart and this is where it's headed. Do us all a favor and don't string her along. A friends with benefits relationship is unfair to her, I won't stand by and allow it to continue."

Now I'm getting pissed. "Axe, no disrespect, but again, we're both adults."

"I'll send her away," he threatens.

"What the fuck is going on here?" Lily asks as she walks into the room. I was so intent on what Axe was saying, I never heard her come through the front door. She glares at her father and says, "Dad, I love you, but you had no right to come here and demand anything." I hang my head when it dawns on me that she heard a helluva lot more than I anticipated.

3

LILY

I stare at the two most important men in my life like they have both lost their ever-loving minds. I'm a grown ass adult and can sleep with whoever I want to sleep with, for fuck's sake! Granted, Maxum has been the only one, and *is* the only one I want, but my dad has no right to come over here and insist he stop seeing me!

Dad doesn't even look embarrassed at me calling him out. No, he's got his president look on and something tells me that I won't like what comes out of his mouth. "Lily, you deserve more than a romp in the sack." He looks pained saying that, but pushes through. "You are an intelligent, smart, beautiful young woman who should be treated like the queen you are, not like a Friday night booty call." If I wasn't so pissed off, I'd laugh at his use of the phrase 'booty call' but I don't want him getting angrier.

"Dad, it's not like that," I protest, glancing at Maxum. He won't meet my eyes and it bothers me a little because despite his hesitance to commit, we get along in every way possible. We're in tune with one another and the fact he isn't looking at me tells me more than I want to know. My dad got to him. *Fuck*!

"It sure as hell looks like it from where all of us are standing," he fires back, glaring at first Maxum, then me. "Do you know what this is doing to your mother?" Great, drag Mom into it to force a guilt trip on me. Newsflash, I'm not packing that bag this time around.

"Considering that it was her who took me to Dr. Bowerman to get on birth control, I think she's fine with it, Dad." My tone is snarky, a disrespectful tone I usually don't show, or use on my dad, but right now, I'm so pissed that I don't care. My body is shaking in aggravation, and my fists are opening and closing, as I attempt to reign in my temper.

"She took you to get you on medicine to help your headaches, Lily. Not so you could engage in bedroom romps." At his words, I roll my eyes, something he hates. Seriously? Bedroom romps? Should I remind him I've already had the birds and the bees talk with him… when I turned twelve!

"Dad, you're sounding suspiciously like one of those real old dudes in the movies that Mom likes to watch. No one says shit like that," I tell him.

When his eyebrow raises I realize I've stepped straight into a blazing inferno. "Lily Callahan, you will show me some respect," he growls out. "I don't care that you're an adult. What I do care about is that your heart is involved, and *he* will most assuredly break it," he continues, pointing to Maxum.

"Isn't that what life's about, Dad? Living, loving, learning? You can't protect me from getting my heart broken, no matter how much you wish you could. This isn't like when I was a little girl and you fixed my toys." I almost feel sorry for him, the look he's giving me is one of a heart-broken father, and all I wanna do is run and wrap my arms around his waist like I used to do when I was a little girl. But, I remember that I'm trying to force him to recognize that I've been on my own for a few years now, and am capable of taking care of myself. All he needs to do is be there for me to lean on when I've been bumped down a peg or two.

His shoulders droop at my words and he looks almost defeated. "I just don't want you hurt, sweetheart," he murmurs, pulling me in for a hug. Despite my anger, I relax in his embrace. He gives the best hugs and I've always felt safe in his arms.

"Daddy, it won't happen," I whisper. I'm making promises that I know deep inside of myself that I can't keep. But, this is all part of growing up and living life. You have to take chances… especially when the heart is involved. Nothing is set in stone, promises have never been made, but a girl can always hope.

"Yeah, baby, it will. You're setting yourself up for something that's likely to crush you and that will kill your mom and me." I'm tired of this conversation already, it's time to let go and let me spread my wings. I want to fly and explore, find myself so to speak. I'm still learning who I am and what I want out of life.

"I'll be fine, Dad. Everything will be fine," I tell him. I try to sound confident, but I suspect he catches the slight tremor in my voice.

Maxum stands and comes to where my dad and I are. Clearing his throat, he says, “Appreciate the visit, Axe. Think Lily and I need to have a chat now.” Dad nods and pulls away after kissing my forehead.

“We’re here, Lily, if you need us,” he says before walking out the door and leaving me with the man who owns me, heart, body, and soul.

I am scared shitless to hear what he has to say. I have a deep, dark feeling he’s fixing to end things and do what my dad accused him of.

Deep breath, Lily. In and out, repeat.

Maxum walks my dad to the door, and after my dad breaches the doorway and he locks the door… it’s deafening. A sound that I’m sure is a preview of what my life is fixing to become.

I’m feeling a bit lightheaded, but assure myself that it can’t be as bad as I’m imagining… right?

Maxum

The silence after Axe leaves is profound. I don’t

know how much she heard, but I don't care to rehash what Axe said. Taking her hand, I lead her over to the couch. "We need to talk," I state. I realize that I was an asshole to Axe and I'll apologize later, but he's right. She deserves more than I can give her and regardless of how well we get along, I need to cut her loose and let her go. Pain radiates in the middle of my chest and I rub at it to try and get it to ease.

"Maxum, I'm sorry he came over like that. He had no right. I'm perfectly content with the way things are between the two of us," Lily states.

She's lying through her damn teeth, and if I were lesser of a man, I'd take what she's offering and run with it.

"We've got a good thing going, you know? We get along, we're good with each other in bed, and can talk about anything. Hell, you like the same shows I do and we even have the same taste in music!" Her eyes are glistening and my heart sits heavy in my chest at the anguish I see on her face.

Fuck, this is harder than I thought it would be. "Lily, baby, he's right. I can't offer what you deserve. You should be more than an occasional fuck. You deserve the entire world; the old lady cut, the ring, the house, the kids — every fucking thing. And I can't give that to you." What I don't say is that I want to, I'd love to hold a mini-Lily in my arms. But I'm not capable and won't even try. I refuse to put an innocent child through what my father put me through. It isn't right to bring a child into this world and not be able to give them one hundred percent of your heart. I don't even know if I have a heart. I live as much of an emotional distance from others as I can… I strive to feel nothing.

"Then why did you start up with me, Maxum? I don't understand! I-I-I always thought things would progress, y'know?" Tears are streaming down her face as she questions me.

I shake my head because when we started, I was driven purely by lust and want. It wasn't until I got to know her that I realized what a gem she truly was; only I'm incapable of giving her a heart that's so damaged, it looks like flayed meat. "Because I wanted you." I know it sounds cruel, but I've never lied to Lily and I won't start now. "You make me hard as fuck and have for a long-ass time and I decided it was time to do something about it."

"B-b-but we are more than just a fuck," she whispers. She stuttered a bit and I'm sure she almost said making love, but she stopped herself.

"Because we're friends, Lily. We just happen to have benefits along with our friendship."

I see a shudder wrack her body and part of me wants to pull her close but that would defeat the purpose of this talk. I need to finish this before I relent and stay in this quasi-relationship we have going on. It's not fair to her and while it guts me to think of her with someone else, if they can give her what I can't, I need to let her go.

But it fucking sucks and I wish I knew where my father was so I could kick his sorry as fuck ass.

"We are friends, Maxum. And sometimes, friends become lovers. I thought that's what we were." Her words sound good in theory, but she has to love herself more than what she's trying to offer me. Her family wants more for her, hell, I want more for her.

"No, we were what your father said." I take a deep breath before saying the words I'm sure will destroy anything we have. "You were nothing more than a booty call, Lily." She gasps, and it takes everything within me not to take the words back, but I need her to hate me enough to leave.

The look she gives me as she stands stabs at me and I resist rubbing my chest again. "I-I won't bother you again, Maxum," she murmurs as she gathers her purse. "I-I'll come into the office and get what I need before you get there, then go work somewhere else so you don't have to see me. Would you mind giving me the key so I can go around your schedule? Please."

I reach out to hand her the key; she shakily snatches it from my hand. I stretch out my hand for her, wanting to hold her one more time in my arms, but she steps back just enough that I'm grasping air. "No, Maxum. You're right. We had fun, it was fun, but now it's time to be adults. We want different things and regardless of whether I love you or not, it takes two to make a relationship. Take care of yourself, Maxum." As she walks out the door, I hear her say, "I love you," so softly it's more of a whisper.

She's gone.

It should be easy to say that because we weren't a real couple, but it's not. Sighing, I head to the fridge and grab another beer.

4

MAXUM

It's been three weeks since I've seen Lily, but she's definitely been around my shop. My office is fully organized and all of my accounts are current. Hell, she's even set up vendor accounts for me so that I can keep my inventory straight. When I see how far in the black I am, I realize that I needed her in here a long time ago. I'm sitting at my desk signing the checks that she's printed out when I notice that there's not a check for her. Fuck that noise; she's the reason I've been able to come in and get caught up on the bigger jobs.

Jaxson found a few people from the local tech school who were near graduation. They work several hours a day, handling basic maintenance shit; like the oil changes that take up too much of my time, and tire rotations. They've made my life so much easier that I contemplate hiring them full time once they graduate. Sometimes, they oversee the state inspections that Texas requires. I pick up the phone and call Cara since she'll know what the going pay rate would be for what Lily is doing.

"Hello?" Her voice is always soothing and I instantly relax.

"Hey, Cara, you got a minute?" I ask.

"Sure. What's up, Maxum?" Her voice cools slightly and I know I have the shit with Lily to thank for that.

"Well, I'm signing checks and shit and there's not one for Lily. What's the going rate to pay someone who does what she does for me?" Even though she's upset with me, I try to act as if nothing is out of the norm. I respect Cara and would hate to lose the motherly type friendship she offers most of us who are orphaned or abandoned by our parents.

"She's pretty much your office manager, correct?" she questions.

"Yeah, she handles the filing and shit, pays the vendors, makes sure the inventory is current and places any orders that are needed."

"I'd think at least twenty-two dollars an hour is fair," she states. I can hear clicking in the background and grin because she probably looked online.

"She's working on the website as well so that customers can schedule times for the basic maintenance," I admit. When Lily emailed me with that suggestion, I talked it over with Jaxson and we decided it would be a great way to ensure we could handle everything. We set up two bays strictly for oil changes and whatnot and put the hours for appointments to correlate when the students are available to work.

"Then you may want to bump it up a little bit," she advises. "Sounds like she's pretty much letting you concentrate on the shop, your customers and the vehicles, while she does all the grunt work behind the scenes."

I nod because that's exactly what has happened. "Should I write a check or do a direct deposit?" I ask. "Jaxson's and my pay are direct deposited."

"I can give you Lily's information since she does the satellite website stuff for all the businesses. She prefers direct deposit so she doesn't have to waste time going to the bank."

I wish she'd said I could write her a check; I miss seeing her smiling face and my chest feels empty since I pushed her away. I resist asking Cara how Lily's doing. Barely. "How many hours do you think?" I feel so fucking clueless with this shit; Jaxson and I know how many hours each job takes and that's how we get paid, but Lily is not here, per se, so I don't know what would be fair.

"I know she comes in every morning around five a.m., scans any paperwork she needs, then proceeds to file it. Then, she heads to the gym and works out, before she heads home. Bandit set up an office for her so she has access to all the files from all of the club businesses."

"Would thirty hours a week be too much? Not enough? I don't want to cheat her, Cara."

"I think thirty hours would be about right, Maxum. I'm sure some weeks she puts in more hours, but there are others where she puts in less. Thirty hours a week is a good average."

I nod even though she can't see me. "Thanks, Cara. Can you email me her direct deposit information? I can input the hours and pay rate into the system and set up an automatic payment." I was so happy when Bandit created the program for me. It allows me to pop in all of our workable hours, does the tax bullshit, sends the monies owed by direct deposit, and then generates a print-out for everyone's records.

Clicking sounds from the phone tell me what she's doing just then and she proves me right when she says, "You've got mail, Maxum."

"Thank you, Cara. You're a lifesaver."

Just a few more seconds and I can get off the phone without asking about Lily.

"She misses you, Maxum. That's all I'll say about it, though. Take care." With that parting shot, she hangs up.

I miss her too.

More than I should, but despite Jaxson yammering at me all the time to get off my ass and claim my woman, I can't. I'm too fucked up.

She didn't seem to care, my subconscious whispers.

Lily

I'VE BEEN AVOIDING ANYWHERE MAXUM WILL BE LIKE THE plague. I can't see him yet; my heart isn't ready. I've cried myself to sleep every single night since we parted ways. My mind races with ways to make him change his mind about me, us, him… all of it. He's worth it, he just needs to come to that realization on his own. Luca called last night. He wants me to come for a visit and spend time with him and Gypsy. I'm seriously considering it. Getting away seems like a good idea. I could use the space and distance from my surroundings. Everything I see, every place I go, I see him, memories of things we did together. I feel like I'm going mad and my headaches have come back full force.

"Earth to Lily." Ralynn dramatically waves her hand in front of my face.

"I'm sorry. What was it you said?" I ask, feeling a bit frazzled.

"I wish I could make this all disappear for you, Lily. What can I do to help you through this?" she questions.

"Can you give me a new head?" I'm only partially joking because even with the Bio-TE, the headaches are breaking through. I've got too much shit to do to be down.

"That shit not working?" she inquires. "I thought they were getting better."

"The doctor said it could take a few treatments before my

levels rose enough to help. But the headaches have gotten worse," I reply. "I max out on the medicine every day."

"I don't think that's healthy, Lil," she cautions. "Have you called the doctor?"

"No, because other than sending me to the hospital for a migraine cocktail, there's not much they can do."

"I know this shit with Maxum isn't helping, either," she states, giving me a look. "Jaxson has tried talking to him, but he keeps saying he's not good enough and has nothing to offer you."

"Rae, I probably sound pathetic saying this, but I'd take him as is, even knowing he can't give me more, if he would just take me back." Tears fill my eyes at my confession because I know I sound like a gutless pussy. But I'm not lying; he's the only one for me.

"Why does that make you sound pathetic? Seriously, Lil, he's been different since y'all split up. I know, I know, the two of you weren't really in a 'relationship' with one another, but all of us feel differently. We saw how he treated you when we were all at the clubhouse. He's attentive and loving, even if he says different."

I close my eyes and take a deep breath at her words. I want to believe them; there's so much hope there and lately, I feel like I'm clinging to my last knot, which is frayed and raggedy. “I can’t think that way, Rae. He made me happy and I know I did the same, but something from his past is keeping him from turning his whole heart over to me.” Tears are pouring down my face and I don’t know if it’s the hammering in my head or the shattering of my heart that has me crying. Lately, I’ve been more emotional than normal, but the doctor did mention that when my hormones start adjusting, I might experience some side effects. Crying jags are apparently one of them, which pisses me off because I’m not normally a crier.

“We’ve got you, Lil. Maybe you need to get away or something,” she says, holding me close.

“Luca called last night and invited me up,” I admit.

“Then you should go. If nothing else, seeing that crazy ass dog should have you laughing, right?” she teases. I grin through my tears because Gypsy’s dog is a little diva with major personality.

“I think you may be right. I just need to disappear from it all. Mom and Dad are driving me insane with trying to set me up on blind dates. They just don’t get it; I don't want anyone other than him. Maybe, I don’t know, maybe I just need to forget about being with my one and settle for the next best thing.”

“You can’t do that to yourself. Don’t give up on finding the right man. Maybe, now hear me out, Maxum wasn't your one, maybe he's just that little girl crush and dream that never went away." I stop and think about her words, it doesn't feel right, but what if she's correct?

"I don't think that's right, my love for him feels real, Rae. He's embedded in my soul; I can't sleep without him invading my dreams. No, he's it for me. It's just a shame I can't be it for him too." I wipe the stray tear that's fallen down my cheek. "It's time for me to admit defeat."

Rae's face falls at my words. "Are you sure? Maybe some time apart will show him that he needs you in his life."

"There's no need pretending something that isn't true, Rae. I'm gonna go to clear my head at Luca's for a while and try to build up a strong, impenetrable wall around my heart. One that Maxum can't break down with his dimples. I'm just so damn tired and drained, Rae."

"Oh, sweetie. Come on, I'll help you pack a few weeks' worth of clothing. But I promise you, if you're gone much longer than that, I'm coming to get you and bring you back home."

"Warning received," I bump her shoulder with mine, "but no promises are being made here today." Other than the stuff that has to be scanned, I can do everything from Luca's. I make a note to ask my mom if she can go by the garage and scan whatever comes in. While I do it every day, she can maybe do it two or three times a week.

“Whatever you say, biotch. I’ll bring you back home kicking and screaming if I must.” I giggle at her proclamation.

“Okay, I’m ready to pack so I can hit the road first thing in the morning.” I’m not convinced that running from my problems is the right thing to do, but it’s what’s best for my mental well-being, so for once, I’m gonna put me first.

5

LILY

I've been on the road for less than an hour and have already had to pull over three damn times. My head hurts, my tummy is turning… I think I'm coming down with the flu or getting a cold. I pull off the next exit when I see a large truck stop and head inside. First order of business is hitting the restroom because the nausea is bad enough, I feel as if I'm gonna puke. I can't take my meds right now either since I'm driving and they tend to knock me out. Once I feel like I can keep going, I grab some ginger ale, a box of saltines, and some over-the-counter pain reliever. It's probably insufficient, but it's better than nothing. "May as well gas up since I didn't do it before I left," I mutter as I get back to the car. When I see that I'm slightly over three-quarters of a tank, I decide to keep going. I've still got about five hours, give or take, before I arrive and I say a silent prayer that my headache doesn't get worse.

BY THE TIME I PULL INTO THE PARKING LOT AT THE clubhouse, I can barely see and I've thrown up several times. "Just get to Luca," I mumble as I pull myself out of the car. "He'll help. He's always helped." I'm just so tired and need to get some rest.

I struggle to open the door but once inside, the darker environment has me sighing in relief. I see Luca sitting at a table and stumble over to him. "Lily?" he asks, standing and walking toward me.

"Hey, Luca," I say.

"You need your meds, don't you?" he questions as he scoops me up and heads to the elevator. I nod, the action causing me to wince. "I got you, Lil, hold on." I don't speak because at this point, most of what I'd say would be gibberish. He pushes the button once we're inside, and I know he's taking me to 'my room' that he insisted be put in when they created the clubhouse. "Yo, Tig," he yells before the elevator doors close, "go grab her shit from her car and haul ass, please."

"You got it, boss man," Tig yells back.

If my head didn't hurt so fucking bad, I'd laugh. The two of them have always been like this; their back-and-forth banter is usually funny, but not today. I hear the clicking of nails when we get to the next floor and the door opens. I guess Lucy has come to greet me too. "God, Luca, hurts," I moan.

"I know, Lil. You should have called me. We'd have come and met you so you could've taken your medicine. You know it's going to be a bitch to get ahead of the pain now."

"Worrywart."

"Don't be a smartass now, Lil. You could've wrecked on the way here and then where would we all be? I'm not fussing. Well, not really, Lily, because I'm sure the shit happening at home isn't helping, but you know better than to let it get this bad."

I close my eyes and turn my head as he reaches my room.

When he opens the door, I see that someone, most likely Gypsy, has refreshed my room and turned the bed down. One of the things I adore about my brother is the fact that in my room, he had those blackout curtains put up so it's nice and dark. If they could talk, my eyeballs would thank him. "Got it, Luca," Tig says, coming in behind us. I hear Lucy's nails hitting the floor and realize that she followed us in as well.

"Let's get you something to drink so you can take your stuff," Luca states. I hear his tone and grin because he sounds a lot like Dad right now.

"Okay, Luca." I know it might take a second dose, but right now, I'm seeking sweet oblivion, so I swallow my pills down and prepare to pass the fuck out.

"We'll talk when you wake up," he states as he leans in and kisses my forehead. "You rest now."

"Love you, bubba," I whisper. We were best friends before we became siblings and he's always been there, watching, protecting, caring.

"Love you more, Lil. More than my bike, more than Lucy, but less than Gypsy," he replies. Glad I'm above the dog at least.

I WAKE TO SOMETHING COLD PROBING MY FACE AND licking my neck. What the fuck? My eyes pop wide open and I sit up quickly in my bed. A woof sound makes me swivel my neck and I laugh at the sight before me. Lucy is on my pillow, tongue lolled out of her mouth and hanging to the left. "Lucy, that's not exactly the way I'd been expecting to wake up," I joke with her as I take my hand and rub her ears. "Are your daddy and momma neglecting your needs, girl?" She woofs again and I burst out into uncontrollable laughter. Don't ask me why this is so funny, but for some reason it's tickled me.

My bladder screams out in agony and I rush from the bed before I pee myself. Lucy, always so protective and attentive, needing attention herself, follows me and watches me as I drop my pants and sit on the toilet. As per her usual, she comes up to me and rubs her head against my knee. This is her way of telling me that since I'm indisposed, I might as well make good use of my hands and fingers and pet her.

"Lily? Is Lucy in there with you?" Gypsy asks through the closed door.

"I'll give you one guess," I chuckle, but never stop rubbing my fingers through her fur. Every time I try to stop, she gives me a whine and I can't resist giving her some more loving.

"That damn dog is always pestering someone or another." I can hear the frustrated breath leave her as she says this to me.

"It's okay, Gypsy. I don't mind, she's actually keeping me company."

"While you take care of business? That's ludicrous, Lily. You shouldn't let her get away with it. Lord only knows Luca would let her get away with murder. He'd even hide the evidence for her." I know she's joking, but I can see this happening, the reality of it is overwhelming. I laugh so hard I begin to leak pee; unwillingly might I add.

"Gypsy! All I'm imagining is Luca giving her a big bone from her prize as he pours lye over a dead body in a dug grave." The visual has me in near hysterics; a far cry from when I got here several hours ago, that's for sure.

"I don't think that vision is too far off," she huffs.

"Give me a few minutes and I'll come down and bring her with me," I holler.

"Sounds good, we have dinner ready when you get down. That's initially what I came in to tell you. Luca insisted that Lucy had run away because I wouldn't give her treats earlier. Wait until I tell him she made her way into your room." Her chuckles follow her out the door and I look down at Lucy and swear I see a glint of mischief in her eyes.

"You were playing hide and seek with your mom to punish her, weren't you?"

"Woof," is her response.

"Damn girl, way to keep your parents on their feet. Give me a high paw five." I hold my hand up, grab her paw, and have them meet in the middle. "Okay, let me wash up and we'll head down to join the others." She gives me a pensive look, huh, guess she's not done punishing Luca and Gypsy as of yet. "You know, you can't hide from them forever, Lucy." I shake my head at the fact I'm talking to a dog, but anyone who's met her soon realizes that she's so much more. She woofs at me and I say, "Don't you sass me, missy. I'll tell your parents."

Her whine has me giggling as we head out of my room and back downstairs. Time to face whatever music Luca plans to play. Knowing him, they made my favorites to butter me up and get me to spill my guts. "I'm on to you, bubba," I whisper as Lucy and I step into the elevator. Once the doors close, I watch as Lucy presses her nose against one of the buttons and we start going down.

"So there you are!" Luca cries out when we reach the bottom and the doors reopen. Is he talking to me? No. No he is not. He crouches down and scoops Lucy into his arms, gets her settled on one side, then tosses his free arm over my shoulder. I catch Lucy licking his jaw and stifle a giggle.

"You thought she ran away, huh?" I ask as we walk toward the kitchen. He sets her down by her food dish and then washes his hands before sitting at the head of the table.

"Why is that so farfetched? Gypsy wouldn't give her any treats after she promised them to Lucy if she was good during her bath." He stares at his old lady and I start laughing at her expression.

"She didn't get any because she was not good, Luca!" Gypsy sighs. "Splashing and whining is not behaving. Don't even get me started on what she did when I clipped her nails, for fuck's sake!" By now I'm holding my arms over my stomach because I'm laughing so hard, it hurts.

"She prefers her nails to be long," Luca replies, taking the platter of meat and putting some on his plate before passing it to me.

"Well, her *mother* prefers them to be short so that she doesn't wear scratches all over her legs and arms," Gypsy hisses. I watch as the canine in question finishes what was in her dish, walks over to where Gypsy sits to Luca's left, glances at Gypsy and then turns her back on her as she lays her head on Luca's foot.

"How's your head?" Luca asks me, effectively changing the subject.

"There's just a slight headache left, bubba," I reply, slowly eating. Sometimes, when I've been as sick as I was earlier, I have a hard time eating. Thankfully, the baked 'fried' chicken, mashed potatoes, and peas that Gypsy made is bland enough that I should be okay.

"You need to take another dose, then," he instructs. I roll my eyes at his president tone; seems he got something from Dad after all! He catches me and I see him hide a grin before he says, "I'm serious, Lil. Don't make me call Mom."

"Fine, fine, I'll do it." If I'm being truthful, I could use the sleep; it's been hit or miss since Maxum and I parted ways.

6

MAXUM

I'm so drunk I can hardly hold my head up. It's Friday night and I joined a few of the guys from the garage for a drink. Well, one drink turned to two and so on. We're all laughing about something that I have no clue about, I'm only going with the flow of the others.

"Maxum, do you see that blonde over there? She can't

keep her eyes off you, man. I swear if you go over there, you may end up leaving with more than just her number," Dustin states. This is one of the men that is working with me from the vo-tech school.

"Not interested," I slur.

"What red-blooded man wouldn't be interested in that? Damn, did you see the size of her jugs?" Vanston whistles.

"Not interested," I once again state.

"Fuck, man. If you're not gonna try to tap that ass, I think I'll give it a shot." Dustin gets up off the stool and walks away. My eyes don't stray to see what direction he's headed, I don't give a fuck what this supposed big breasted blonde looks like… she's not my blonde after all.

"You look like someone's spit on your grave. What gives?" Vanston asks. What, does he think, because I've shared a few beers with him and let him work as an intern in my garage that I need to spill my guts? What, are we BFFs now? Yeah, I don't think so.

"None of your business." I lean over to make sure and look him in the eye, instead I end up swaying on my stool and nearly fall off.

"Wow, maybe it's time for you to call it a night?" Vanston expresses.

"May..." I hiccup, "maybe-be you need to mind your own damn business." I know I'm being a bit of a dick, but I'm a miserable son of a bitch.

"Hey, Max. You need a ride home, man?" I feel a hand clutch my shoulder. I look over and see my brother, Hatch, giving me a look that says I need to heed his suggestion and run with it.

"Sure," I slur. Damn, my tongue feels swollen and heavy. I stand and sway into him, he reaches his arms up and stops me from falling face first into him.

"Damn, dude, I had no idea you felt that way," he teases me. For some damn reason, I find this the funniest thing I've heard all night and laugh so hard that I have to look down and make sure there's not a wet spot on my jeans. I begin bouncing from foot to foot in a need to go use the restroom but not sure how I'd make it there on my own.

"Is that your version of the peepee dance?" Hatch raises his eyes from my feet to my eyes as he asks this. I would laugh again, but I would embarrass the fuck out of myself so I stay quiet.

"Yep, there a bush nearby?" I question. Every drink I ingested has apparently reached my bladder and things could get dicey if I don't hit the head soon.

"If not, man, I'm sure there's a hydrant out there somewhere," he chuckles.

"I'm not a damn dog, man." I stop and think about the words that just left my mouth.

"Could've fooled me." For the first time, I see that he's not really happy with me, but he's here doing his brotherly duty. I hate feeling like I'm someone else's responsibility.

"What-what's that supposed to mean?" I angrily spit out the question.

"Nothing. I'm not having a conversation of this magnitude with you while you're drunk off your ass." He grabs my arm and all but drags me toward the front door. As much as I try, I can't get my feet to work correctly and it pisses me the hell off.

"Dammit!" I yell out.

"What?" He turns around and I can see his enforcer defensive side come out, ready for a threat to attack us.

"My damn feet are numb and aren't working!" Can't he tell? I mean, I'm stumbling into him more than I'm putting one foot in front of the other.

"Seriously, Max? Are you trying to give me a fucking heart attack? DJ would have your ass if she had to get out of bed and come sit at the damn hospital all night." He shakes his head in disbelief at my outburst.

I shudder because even as drunk as I am, the thought of Donna Jo Hatchet anywhere near me, knowing how she feels about Lily, scares the fuck out of me. I've tried keeping my head down when I'm at the clubhouse, but I can feel the censuring looks and condemnation that rolls off of not only the women, but my own damn brothers. "Guess I had more than I should have, Hatch," I mumble.

"Been happening a lot lately, brother," he notes as he gets me to his truck. "Fuck, hang on, walk to the other side and take a piss, just don't do it by my door."

I stumble around to the back of the truck and take a piss, my bladder sighing in relief. Once done, I tuck myself back into my jeans and somehow manage to get myself into the passenger side of the truck. Leaning my head back, I sigh. I'm too tired and drunk to carry on any sort of intelligent conversation right now, but something tells me that I'll be doing more listening than talking.

Hatch gets in and leans over to buckle my seat belt. When I try to protest, he raises his eyebrow at me and states, "Safety first, brother, and you don't look like you're in any shape to do it yourself." I shrug and let him do what he feels is necessary, unwilling to expend the energy it would take me to argue. With his truck now in gear, he points it toward my apartment before he starts talking. "You look like shit, Maxum. You're drinking too much, you've lost weight, and your attitude, quite frankly, fucking sucks."

"Don't hold back, Hatch, tell me how you really feel," I say. I've known this was coming, I just wasn't sure who was going to draw the short straw, so to speak. I've been surly and almost nasty to the guys at the shop, which is another reason we're closed tomorrow. I think everyone needs a day away from me. Me, on the other hand? I'm stuck with my fucking thoughts and they keep spinning around one thing — Lily.

"Not planning to. You need to get your shit in order and figure out what you want."

"I *wanted* things to stay the way they were." My words are still slurred, but I can feel the rage that's been simmering below the surface rising and I know if I were in my right mind, I wouldn't be telling Lily's uncle that I was content with a booty call from his niece. However, the alcohol has dulled my brain significantly, and I completely miss the fist that flies toward me, catching me in the cheek. "Fuck, Hatch! What the fuck did you do that for?" Tears sting my eyes at the onset of pain and I glare at him, only to see his face hard as if it's set in stone.

"That's my niece, your *president's* daughter that you're talking about like she's no better than a whore." What? I'd never talk about Lily like that; she was a virgin when she came to me and unless she's found someone else in just a few short weeks, I'm the only one she's been with intimately.

"I didn't say that, Hatch," I protest, my hand rubbing at my cheek. I suspect I'll have a helluva bruise because he didn't pull back on that punch.

"Yeah, you did, brother. By saying you were content with things the way they were, you were saying she's not good enough for more than an occasional romp."

"*I'm* not good enough for her, Hatch," I admit. "Had to let her go, no matter how good we got along and I ain't talking about in bed." Another thing I miss, our movie nights, and how she would curl into me as we would quote lines from our favorites.

"Good, because as far as I'm concerned, she's still that little girl with pigtails in her hair, not a grown ass woman who has stupidly fallen for a brother who has issues committing."

"You don't understand, brother." Maybe it's the alcohol. Maybe it's because I'm tired of being misunderstood when it comes to my issues with relationships. But suddenly it all comes pouring out of me. "My old man was a prick and a bastard. Treated me and my ma like shit up to, and including, the day she left for good, leaving me with him. He told me that relationships weren't worth it; that fucking them and letting them go was the way to be."

We've reached my apartment and he parks before getting out of his truck and helping me out. I'm thinking the last three beers and two shots weren't my wisest decision because it seems to take forever to get up the stairs. He helps me in, then closes and locks the door while I stumble to the couch, kicking my boots off along the way. "Hold that thought, brother," Hatch states, before walking into my kitchen. I hear the refrigerator door open, then several cabinets are opened and closed before he returns, holding out a bottle of water in one hand and several pills in the other. "Figure you need to start hydrating and take something for that fucking headache you're going to have tomorrow," he says in response to my unasked question.

"Thanks, Hatch." I thankfully accept the offer. A hangover headache is a bitch to get past. Not to mention, the spinning of a room and barfing into the porcelain throne… none of which I'm looking forward to experiencing.

He sits down on the loveseat opposite from me and I brace myself for whatever he's about to say. "Maxum, you're one of my brothers and you've been a good one since you patched into the club. You've watched each of us find someone and settle down, right?" At my nod, he continues,

"Why don't you think you deserve the same? Fuck, you know some of your brothers have been in worse situations growing up and they're happy as pigs are when they get a chance to play in the mud. It's not all sunshine and roses; we all have disagreements with our women, but we love, respect and treasure them first and foremost. And, Maxum? I've seen, fuck, we've *all* seen how you are around Lily. The two of you practically glow or some shit when you're together. How can you think that she's only good for a casual fuck?"

"She deserves better," I insist. This is something I continually repeat to myself and anyone who's asked about her and me. How can they not see the dirt that layers my body, heart and mind? It's all over me, I'm coated in it, I see it clearly every single time I look at myself in a mirror.

"Better than what? Better than a man who'd lay his life down for her? Better than a man who supports whatever she wants to try? Better than a man who's spent his fair share of time taking care of her when she's down with one of her headaches? I don't think so, brother. I think I'm staring at the best man for her, and it's time you woke up and smelled the coffee and got with the fucking program. Do you really want to go the rest of your life without her in it? Not see her smile, hear her laugh? I'm not gonna discuss the sex aspect because I watched her grow up, but there's more to life than sex, and from where I sit, the two of you have built a helluva foundation based on trust, honesty, and loyalty. You need to straighten shit out in your head and then go get your woman because right now, she's vulnerable to anyone who comes along since she doesn't think you give two fucks about her."

I slump even further into the couch at his words. I wasn't expecting this, for him to calmly discuss the situation with me. I figured he'd knock me around some, yell about hurting his niece, then leave me laying in a puddle of drool. "I think it's too late, Hatch," I mutter. There's a strange sensation in my chest and I don't have the mental capacity to examine it too closely right now.

But it feels suspiciously like… *hope.*

7

MAXUM

The pounding making itself known in my head is only temporarily superseded by the banging on the fucking door. "Go away, I'm sleeping!" I holler from my position on the couch. After Hatch said his piece, he left me there, and I never managed to make it to the bed. I fell asleep with his words ringing in my head and now, with the hangover from hell, as well as whoever the fuck is at my door, everything is simply too much.

"Answer the fucking door, asshole!" Fuck. It's Jaxson and he won't go away, he's one hardheaded mother-fucker when he wants to be. Cursing a blue streak that would make any sailor proud, I stumble while getting up. When I finally make it to the front door, I unlatch the chain then unlock the bottom lock. I open my front door with gusto ready to chew his ass out but stop my tirade when both Jaxson and Talon push their way through. I throw my hands up in the air… might as well give the fuck up. I have no chance between the two of them.

"What the fuck? This ain't Grand Central Station. Last I knew, it was perfectly fine for a guy to lie around and do nothing." The smell of coffee increases as Jaxson shoves a cup in my hands. Normally, the shop is open on Saturdays, but with the interns, we're caught up and I decided we needed to take the day off. Well, that and the fact that I've been such a surly bastard, even I can't stand myself.

"Drink this, brother. Hatch said you needed us so we're here," he says as Talon sets down a bag full of donuts. My stomach rolls at the scent of fresh java and the icing on the donuts.

"What the fuck?" I ask. Before either of them can answer, I

head into the kitchen and grab some more aspirin, as well as another bottle of water.

“Guess he figures that since we’re all the best of friends, and the three of us are closest in age, that we can help unfuck your head or something,” Talon says around a mouthful of donut. I feel my stomach cringe and realize that I probably shouldn’t eat just yet.

“Jesus fucking Christ. Y’all gonna braid my hair next?” I ask. At Jaxson’s smirk, I throw one of the pillows that Lily helped pick out at him. “Shut it, asshole. I’m fine, it’s all fine.” Secretly, even though I’m hungover, it touches me that the two of them are taking one of their only days off to be with me instead of their old ladies. Not gonna say anything, though; I’m no pussy.

“If it’s so fine, why’s Lily up with Luca and Gypsy? Why’ve you been walking around like a surly bear who got shot in the ass with a BB gun? We know shit wasn’t all that great for you growing up. Hell, man, I think most of us have fucked up histories. But since we all came into the Rebel Guardians family, have you ever seen any one of our other brothers treat any of the women horribly? No, you haven’t and if nothing else, ditch the shit you grew up with and fill it with those memories. Lily loves you, brother, and if you were honest with yourself, you’d realize that you love her too,” Talon states. He’s usually somewhat quiet but apparently, in this 'Let's Help Maxum Get His Head Out Of His Ass' quest, he's taken a vow of verbal vomit or some shit. "Don't push her so far away that you don't get her back. I nearly lost Claree doing that shit, brother, and I won't let you do it to yourself or to Lily."

I drop my head in my hands at his words. "Y'all have no clue, no idea at all about the fucking monsters I deal with thanks to my dad. Until my mom left when I turned sixteen, I was regularly screamed at, beaten, and treated like I was a waste of space with no redeeming qualities. When my mom left, it got worse. If what my parents had was love, I don't want any part of it." I probably sound like a pussy right now, but I remember shaking beneath the covers as a kid while the screams and thumps against the wall went on, night after night. Hell, it's one of the reasons I typically don't drink all that much because that's what *he* would do and I don't wanna be like my old man.

"Fuck, man, you've been holding this shit in for a long ass time," Jaxson mutters. "Why didn't you ever say something before? We would've helped you fight those demons and put them to rest."

"Because I've never intended to take an old lady, brother. Was just gonna take what I could get when I needed it from anyone willing," I reply.

"And then along came Lily," Talon says in understanding,

giving me a knowing look. Fucker. He knows I've been drawn to her for more years than I wanna think about.

"Yeah," I sigh. "But I think I fucked it all up six ways from Sunday and there's no coming back from the shit I said." It sounds like all I'm doing is coming up with excuses, but that couldn't be further from the truth. Facts are facts, and it's a given that I pushed her away and hurt her more than any love she could potentially still feel from me could overcome.

"Do you not know Lily? Cause brother, you sure aren't acting like you do," Jaxson asks, laughing. "She's one of the most forgiving, caring people I know."

That spark of hope ignites once again at his words but I try to tamp it down. "You're still gonna have to work hard to get her back, brother," Talon cautions. "She's not a pushover by a long shot, even if she is one of the sweetest people I've ever known."

"I can't afford to fuck things up, y'all. Axe would kill me if I hurt her more than I've already done. Hell, *Cara* would probably do the deed," I state.

"Then we need to find you someone you can talk to, besides us that is, so you can get your head on straight," Jaxson replies. The look he gives me lets me know that this isn't something I can just push to the side.

"At the risk of sounding like a fucking chick, fine," I grumble. "Not sure how talking to someone would help." Do bad ass bikers talk to counselors? Fuck if I know, but if it helps me get Lily back and keep her forever, I'd be willing to do about anything to make that happen. I still don't think I'll ever be good enough for her, but I'm feeling a bit selfish. I have missed the ever-loving fuck out of her since we parted ways.

"I promise, brother, it helps. Look at Rae. You work on yourself, let the rest of us worry about Lily," Jaxson says. When that flicker of hope sparks again, I decide that I should embrace the flames and see where it takes me.

Lily

Standing outside of the clubhouse, I'm laughing my ass off at Maddox and Luca as they banter back and forth. Tig's head is bouncing back and forth like a ping-pong ball. If I'm being completely honest, he looks sad that they won't let him get a word in edgewise.

"Why are you two mad at me?" Tig pouts and crosses his arms across his chest.

"Ain't no one mad at you, Tig. Everything isn't always about you." Luca rolls his eyes in response.

"It is in my world," Tig shouts.

"Hey, where's Danika?" I ask him. He turns around, gives me a glaring look then turns and stomps away.

"Hey! How'd you do that? I need to learn all of your tricks," Luca laughs. "I've been trying to get him to get lost for nearly an hour now. I'm jealous of your skills, little sister."

I roll my eyes because we're technically the same age. "All I did was ask him about Danika," I admit. "I thought they were… uh… getting close. At least that's what it seemed like the last time I was here visiting."

"Yeah, I have absolutely no clue what the hell happened there, and he sure as fuck won't talk to me about it at all. Good going, though. Hey, I had an idea for you," Luca says. "Since you keep hogging my dog, what if we go look for one for you since you're a single woman living on her own? Well, not totally on your own while you're here, but you know what I mean."

I'm about to reply when I hear, "Watch out! Shit! Fuck! Y'all move!" screamed from the roof of the clubhouse and look up in time to see a small bundle of shingles sliding off the edge of the roof. Before I can move, I feel the impact against the back of my head and I fall forward, face planting in the grass. I hear Luca and Maddox screaming my name as the darkness engulfs me.

WAKING UP, I REALIZE QUICKLY THAT I'M IN THE hospital. My head feels like I've got the whole percussion section of the New York Symphony in it, pounding away so hard that just moving my head a little bit has me swallowing back bile. I see Luca asleep in the chair, my hand loosely clasped in his, with Gypsy curled around him. When my eyes meet my mom's, I gasp, causing Luca and Gypsy to both wake up.

"Oh, thank God, Lily," Mom cries out, coming over to my side and reaching out to smooth back my hair. I melt into her embrace, just as I've always done, but I hate that they've had to come all this way over a little bump on the head. Plus, this makes me worry. If they know, does *he* know? If so, why isn't he here too?

"Luca? Why did you call Mom and Dad?" I ask, my voice raspy from disuse.

"Lily, you've been unconscious for days! There's no fucking way I wasn't going to let them know that you'd been hurt," he replies before grabbing a cup filled with water. He holds the straw up to my lips and I take a few swallows, grateful for the soothing feel of the cold water as it slides down my throat. I didn't realize how parched I was and I greedily suck it down until Luca pulls it away, saying, "Not so fast, Lil. I'll give you more in a little bit."

"Days?" How the hell have I slept for days? All I can seem to remember is being in the courtyard at Luca's clubhouse; like a whisper in my head, I remember someone scream from above us to *watch* out, then the memory overcomes me as I remember that something actually hit me… hard. Everything else is a dark, blank void, buried deep inside of my memory bank… one that I hope stays hidden in time, if the looks on my family's face is any indication of what I've suffered.

"Yeah, honey, days. Gypsy called while Luca rode with you in the ambulance since he pretty much knows your medical history. Your dad and I packed a bag, sent the twins to your Aunt DJ and Uncle Hatch, then we hit the road a few minutes later." My eyes widen because my mom is a lot of things, but spontaneity isn't really a strong point. She's a planner, using lists full of bullet points to ensure she accomplishes her goals and she regularly sets herself tasks to accomplish. When she sees my non-verbal response, she chuckles then says, "We shopped for what we needed when we got here, sweetheart. Whatever we left behind; we now have. Lord only knows our heads were jumbled as we tried to remember all of the necessities. Needless to say, we left with a few essentials missing. You should've seen your dad, he was like a raging bull, hollering at me to hurry my butt up, we could get whatever we needed when we got here." Visually, I can see all of this taking place in my head... but, I can't fathom my father using the word butt... in this instance it was more like ass, but Mom still can't bring herself to use 'inappropriate' words.

God, I love my parents. I know that biologically, Cara isn't my mom, we don't share the same blood, but she came into my life when I was six and has been the only mom in my life. I couldn't have asked for a better woman to come into my life, step into the role she did, and unite us as a family. She's never treated me any differently from Luca or the twins. Nope, in Caraleigh Callahan's eyes, I'm hers, plain and simple.

"W-what's wrong with me?" I stutter out, holding the tears at bay that want to slip free. I don't want to worry anyone with my emotional outburst. My heart and soul are damaged, and it's not their place to glue everything back together again. I feel like Humpty Dumpty right about now.

"Where do I start? When you fell, you face planted and neither me nor Maddox were close enough to catch you, so you managed to break your own damn nose," Luca states. "The stack of shingles fell and hit you in the back of your head, so you've got a large gash back there that required twenty stitches. Apparently, you subconsciously threw your arms out when you fell and managed to break your left wrist and sprain your right one. You have a grade three concussion, too, which is why your head is probably killing you." I didn't want to mention the marching band that's sharing headspace with me, but yeah, my head is aching and I could use a Tylenol… something. It could also explain the light sensitivity I'm suffering. The list is ever growing of the pains racking my body at this moment.

Damn, all I can think of right now is that because I couldn't get out of the way, leaping tall buildings in a single bound, that I am the unluckiest girl on the planet. I need a Midol, I'm having an emotional breakdown, only I don't want to show that since everyone is already concerned enough about me. I'm about to ask something else when Mom gives Luca a perturbed look, he shoots one back at her before standing up and stretching his arms above his head. He then ends up reaching his hand out and taking Gypsy's in his, then silently begins walking away taking my soon-to-be sister-in-law with him. "I'll go look for Dad and let him know she's awake," he says over his shoulder to Mom. She nods and comes to sit in the chair where Luca was recently sitting. What I really wish she'd do is climb into bed with me, hold me tightly to her, and reassure me everything wrong in my world will be alright. But I won't ask that of her, she looks stressed enough as it is.

"Mom? Is there something else?" I ask, remembering the scathing look she sent in my brother's direction when he was opening his mouth to tell me something. Something that seemed important. It was odd that Mom shut him up with one look alone… my big, badass biker brother, can still be brought to his knees by our mother… and his woman, it seems.

She closes her eyes and takes a deep breath. "Yeah, my Lily Bug, there is. Sweetheart, you're pregnant." Umm… excuse me? Did she just say what I think she did? Surely not… there's no way that could be possible! I've obviously suffered a major head trauma because I could have sworn she said I was pregnant.

"Mom, that can't be possible," I insist. I've only ever been with Maxum, and we were careful. Always using precaution… he was so scared that this would come to fruition that he even checked my birth control pills. I don't know why the possibility of pending fatherhood had him so scared, but any time the topic would come up, he'd turn white as a sheet and begin shaking… almost as if fear blanketed the rational part of his brain.

Her raised eyebrows have me gulping. "Lily, I know you

know how babies are created and conceived. You've had the birds and bees talk with your dad. I also know that you and Maxum, until recently, have been in an intimate relationship." My eyes close in humiliation from her acknowledging this. How embarrassing, please, earth, open up and swallow me into the pits of hell! There are some topics meant to be discussed with parents, and those that shouldn't… in my mind, this is one of those instances that should *not* be talked about.

"Mom, I'm on the pill! And… until the last time, he also used condoms," I defend vehemently. "How could this even be a possibility?" I haven't been ill or taken any sort of medication that would lessen my birth control's effectiveness, so I'm baffled at what she's told me. We need to ask for further testing, my labs must've gotten mixed up with someone else's and they've given us false results… yeah, we'll go with that for my peace of mind.

"It just is, Lil. I'm going to forewarn you, though, that your father is equal parts ecstatic over our first grandchild and pissed at Maxum for his recent behavior, especially with all the things he's done where you're concerned," she emphasizes.

Great. That's just great, it's all I need on top of everything else. I won't get Braxton, the awesome, funny dad. No, I'll get Axe, the mean as fuck MC president. Son of a fucking bitch, fucking hell that hole can open up right now! I sigh then drop my head. "I'm sorry, Mom. Never expected this to happen." Disappointing my parents, aunts, and uncles, bothers me. I've never done well with upsetting any of them. I've strived to be the good girl.

"It's not like you're a sixteen-year-old teenager, sweetheart. You're an adult who makes enough money to support yourself as well as a child on your own. It won't be easy, but you know we'll all help as much as we can." The image of me sitting in a rocking chair, with a screaming baby as tears fall, overwhelms me. I never wanted to be a single mom, I always envisioned a loving man beside me as I fed our baby the nutrients he or she needed from my breasts. Now, all I can see is me alone, depressed and scared.

Let the good times roll.

I feel the tears trickling down my face. "How do I tell Maxum?" I whisper. "He didn't want me before, he's going to think I did this on purpose to trap him! No, no, no. I'm not saying anything and none of you can either!" Fear is taking hold, he'll hate me, us, I can't deal with that right now… maybe never. "I'll just stay up here a little longer. I can work from the clubhouse just fine, as long as you're still willing to go to the office and scan the paperwork for me." The longer I think about it, the more positive I am this is the way it needs to happen.

"I don't like it, Lily. He has a right to know," she cautions me.

"I'll tell him, eventually, Mom. Just… not right now, okay?" After the stuff he said, I'm not sure how to face him to drop this bombshell on him. I start to say something else when my dad walks in the room, looking almost defeated. "Dad?" I whisper. "Are you okay?" I'm pretty positive I know the answer to this but ask it anyway.

He walks over and sits on the side of the bed and takes my semi-good hand in his. "Lily, I just don't know what to do with all of this," he admits. "Part of me wants to beat the shit out of my brother for putting you in the position of being a single mom, but the other part of me is trying hard to remember that the two of you are adults who need to work this shit out on your own, without any interference from outside sources. But as your dad, this is hard to let go of. I vowed the day you were born and I saw you for the first time that I'd protect you from all harm." I remember the story that Aunt Paisley told about how she took care of me until Dad came home. She says it was love at first sight when he saw me. After the shock of finding out he was a father, and my mother disappearing, leaving me behind that is.

All I can do is nod because I've managed to toss a wrench into the brotherhood and I wasn't even trying. "I'm sorry, Dad. It shouldn't have happened, though. We were cautious and used protection," I vow.

"Well, as Nan has always stated, children are never to be viewed as a mistake. The circumstances might not be the best, but they're always blessings. We'll make the best of it, sweetheart," he tells me.

"I'm going to stay up here for a while," I admit to him. When he gives me a look, I continue, "Just until I can figure out how to tell Maxum the news, Dad. He deserves to know but we didn't exactly leave things on the best of terms." I feel more tears slide down my face, struggling to not completely break down in front of him. I'm going to be a mom! It's time to pull up my big-girl britches and face shit head on, without hiding behind my parents. "I'm self-sufficient, so even if he doesn't want anything to do with me, I can support myself and my baby. Y'all made sure all of us kids could take care of ourselves. But I'll need to get more clothes and stuff up here." The last part is me thinking and rattling words out loud, I didn't mean they had to figure this out for me, I'm just problem solving in my head but verbalizing things as they hit.

"I'll get some more of your things packed, Lily. Well, since I'm here, I'll see if Rae and Claree can do it, if that's okay," Mom interjects. That could work and be beneficial to us all. That way, my folks will be here to help me settle in and come to terms with the news that is still hard to believe.

"I'm fine with that, Mom. Thank you."

8

MAXUM

I'm once again sitting at the bar at the clubhouse, having a much-needed beer when I overhear something that has my heart clenching. "What did you just say?" I ask Ralynn. My body poised for running, surely my brain is intoxicated by beer suds and I didn't hear what I think I did.

She glances at me and I see her eyes narrow briefly before she masks her expression. “Lily is going to stay with Luca and Gypsy while she heals,” she says. My hackles rise, my hands involuntarily clench into fists as she says this so nonchalantly to me. If she wasn’t a club member’s old lady and Hatch’s daughter, I’d ring her damn neck. She’s always been a sassy little thing, but now isn’t the time to portray that attitude.

“Heals from what?” My heart is now hammering profusely in my chest as I feel sweat begin to bead on my forehead. Lily was hurt? Why didn’t anyone tell me? Fear wars with rage and I find myself fighting the urge to keep from punching a hole in the wall. Nan would have my ass for messing up her well-thought-out decorating.

“She, uh…” She looks around the room for someone to step in and help her. “Lily had a mishap at the clubhouse late last week,” she stammers out.

Claree eventually pipes into the conversation and adds what she knows. “Spent a few days in the hospital and is now recovering at their clubhouse. I got some of her stuff packed up, as soon as Talon arrives, we’re planning to drive up and drop off her belongings while Mom and Dad watch the kids.”

I don’t even think about what I’m saying. “I’ll take it,” I

say to the two of them. I may not be what she needs, but I have to put my eyes on her to make sure she's okay.

Both of their eyes widen comically at my outburst. "A-are you sure, Maxum? We don't mind at all," Claree stammers out.

"Easier for me to do it so y'all don't have to uproot the kids," I justify.

"Mom and Dad don't mind watching them," she states. "And it would give us a little break, plus I need to see her for myself."

"Same," I mutter.

"Well, how about this—why don't you come along? I'm sure she'd want to see you." She chews on her bottom lip as the last words leave her. She and I both are nervous, wondering if her words hold any merit of truth.

Yeah, I bet I'm the last fucking person she wants to see, especially if she's been hurt. Someone needs to hide any and all sharp instruments from Lily when I enter the same room as her. "That's a good idea, brother," Hatch interjects, coming up behind us. Apparently, he just so 'happened' to be within eavesdropping range, overhearing enough of our conversation, adding in his two-cents mind you, that he knows we're talking about Lily.

"You think so, Hatch?" Ever since he, Jaxson, and Talon had their talk with me, I've been seeing a local therapist. I wasn't fully sold on having a female to talk to, but she's helping me unravel the shit in my head. I get homework every week, and while I sometimes feel like a weak-ass pussy, I have an end goal in mind so I do it. I am determined to come out the victor, leaving my father's words of 'wisdom' behind in the dust.

"Yeah, I do, but you can always make a phone call and double-check," he replies, giving me a look. Is he trying to tell me to call, or not? I can't decipher if he's setting me up, or trying to help me out. He's a hard man to read, which isn't helping me out in the decision-making process here.

"Wait, is that where Axe and Cara have been?" I knew they'd been gone for about a week, but just presumed that they had decided to take a mini-vacation or something. Since my 'talk' with Axe, I've been keeping a low profile. I know I've disappointed him and the other brothers and all I can say is, I'm trying. It's not a lie, although, I haven't gone to him and told him as much.

"Yeah, they took off pretty much after getting the call," Rae states. "Shocked the hell out of Lily, that's for sure, since Cara is usually so organized," she says on a snort which has her dad slipping out a small laugh.

I chuckle because after all the years of being around her, that's something I know first-hand. Cara is almost OCD about certain things and when it comes to trips, she's usually got her suitcase packed at least a week ahead of time. "I-is she okay?" I question.

"She messed herself up pretty good, actually," Rae says. "Broken nose, broken wrist, stitches in the back of her head, nasty concussion." I send a bold, scathing look in Hatch's direction. I find it amusing that all of a sudden his boots need a closer inspection.

"What in the *fuck* happened?" There's nothing I can think of that would cause injuries to the front and back. I refuse to examine how my voice sounds nearly panicked. Closing my eyes, I count to ten. When that doesn't work, I expand it to twenty. One of the coping techniques the therapist is assisting me with.

"Some of Maddox's crew were replacing shingles on the leaking rooftop of their clubhouse when part of a bundle slipped, falling from the stack, smacking her in the back portion of her head. She fell forward, and apparently tried to break her fall by using her hands to support her, sprained one and broke the other," Hatch states. "Gave her a pretty good concussion too; she was unconscious for almost three days." *Three days!* That's a long period of time to lose consciousness for.

Jesus mother*fucking* Christ. Lily was badly hurt; yet, every one of my *brothers* and friends had the audacity to keep this from me! What, no one had the thought that it would matter to me? Every single one of them knows how I feel about her. I've been open and honest with them in that regard, I'm working hard to be the man she deserves. I push down the anger that comes roaring from deep within to the forefront. I'm sure they were just protecting Lily but that doesn't ease my fears any. I'm a bit hurt, but I'm also trying to understand where they were coming from. But that voice in my head reminds me that loyalty to me isn't what I thought it was. We're brothers, we're supposed to be there for each other and share important information. For the first time since joining RGMC, I feel left out, an outsider, something my father always warned me about.

I've only got myself to blame.

I put my trust in someone other than me. All the work I've done comes crashing down over me in waves.

If I can't believe in the brotherhood, who can I trust?

I shake those feelings of betrayal away. Without another word, I step outside and pull my phone from my pocket. A phone call with my therapist is needed. I'm desperate for someone to help me figure out the jumbled emotions running rampant in my brain. Bandit found me a therapist who specializes in childhood abuse. It's someone different than Rae used, which put me at ease. I wanted someone who didn't counsel my friends. I needed someone with fresh eyes, to be my sounding board when I needed it.

"Dr. Graves," she answers. She's a sweet older woman, the grandmotherly type.

"It's Maxum. Do you have time for a quick chat?" I ask her.

"I'm in between patients right now so it's a great time to talk," she sweetly states.

"I've got some shit running through my head and it's leading me in a direction I don't wanna go," I admit.

"Tell me what's going on with you today." She has that tone in her voice that lets me know she's intently ready to doctor me. I rattle out every conversation I've had and what I'm thinking in regard to my brothers.

"Let me ask you a question. Do you think they set out to betray you? Is it possible that they were stuck between a rock and a hard place? From what you've shared with me when it comes to them, they seem more loyal to you than you are to yourself." This makes me stop and think.

"Lily is my president's daughter," I say out loud. "I don't know, all I can hear is my father's voice telling me that no one cares about me, that I'm only passing time, I'm no more than a pet they have to care for."

"No offense, Maxum, but your father is a nuisance that doesn't deserve space in your head."

"I know, but I can't help the ghosts that plague me," I reiterate.

"If you had a daughter, Maxum. What would you have done in this instance?" she questions.

"The same thing," I hesitantly admit.

"Then that's what you need to think about when these feelings overcome you. Put yourself in someone else's shoes, think of how you'd react, and let that lead you to how you're feeling on the subject."

"Thanks, Doc. I needed to hear that."

"Don't hesitate to call me any time. Day or night; you can do this, Maxum. Have faith in yourself and those around you. They are your family; your dad, he's a blip on the radar."

Lily

No one has given me any time alone to adjust to my new, upcoming life. I know everyone means well, but it's grating on my last nerve. I've managed to escape into my room here at Luca's clubhouse, but I know my peaceful existence is only for a short time period. Mom has literally fluffed my pillows every night before I sleep and my dad has been underfoot every time I roam around.

I'm feeling suffocated and want to scream each time I see the two of them. Is it too much to ask to use the restroom by myself? It's not as if I can harm myself or my unborn child sitting on the toilet for Christ's sake.

A knock on my door has me groaning before hollering, "It's open!"

"Oh good, you're awake. I didn't want to disturb you if you were sleeping," Mom says as she barrels into the room. I put a pillow over my face and force the scream that wants to escape me to the back of my throat. "Don't do that, Lil. You won't get the oxygen your body needs." Rolling my eyes, I remove said pillow from my face.

"What's up, Mom?" I ask even though all I want to do is order her away from the only place I can come to escape the madness.

"Just heard from Claree. She, Talon, Rae, Jaxson and Maxum are on their way with your belongings." The last name she sped through. Surely she didn't say *he* was coming.

"Mom!"

"Don't you Mom me in that voice, Lily Callahan." She scolds me as she places her closed fists on her hips. "I said it was okay, you've hidden from him long enough, young lady. You two are grown-ups and have a little one on the way that needs both of you. Don't be a coward, you can do this."

Coward. Me? He's the one who ran from me… from us. And she has the audacity to call me a coward? "He's the coward," I mumble like a sullen child.

"Lily. This isn't something either of you can run from. You were both in that bed and you both need to face the consequences. Your father and I have abided by your wishes, but it's time. Maxum needs to know, come to grips with the fact that his life is forever about to change. You owe this to that baby growing in your belly. He or she has a right to have their father in their life. I know this is hard on you, but this isn't just about you or him anymore. It's time you both face your fears and talk things out. If y'all can make a good thing come of this and be together, that's splendid, if not, that's okay too, as long as your baby grows up loved by both of you, it's all that matters."

"I don't think I can be around him when he finds his one," I admit.

"This frame of thinking is you basing it on the presumption that his *one* isn't you." She gives me a deadpan look.

"I know I'm not. He threw me away so easily, that there's no way I'm his heart and soul." Saying this out loud has me grieving what should've been. I love him so much that the thought of him with someone else causes my heart to shatter into a million fractured pieces.

"Honey, that boy has demons he needs to face. Do that with him, show him there's someone willing to fight for and with him." Her advice has merit, I'll admit, but I don't want to be the only one fighting for us. It's not fair for anyone to ask me to do that. "You have about an hour to pull yourself together. I came to give you the news and let you process. I'll send him right up before your dad and brother get a chance to get their hands on him," she says, as she turns on the heels of her feet and leaves the room as quickly as she came in.

I haven't even let the fact set in that I'm gonna be a mom, now I have to tell Maxum he's gonna be a dad. This day just keeps getting better and better as the minutes roll by.

9

MAXUM

My head is all over the place as we ride toward Fallen Creek. I'm sure I'll have to deal with Luca's attitude, as well as Axe's wrath. But Dr. Graves' words keep ringing in my head and if it means I have to open myself up to them, I'll do it. Right now, I need to put my eyes on Lily and reassure myself that she's going to be okay.

She's my best friend outside of Jaxson. I never thought I'd have a female for a friend, not with the way my dad poisoned me. Yet somehow, she crept underneath the barriers I've erected all my life and made herself at home.

"What am I gonna do if she's not willing to wait while I get my shit straight?" I mutter to myself. I honestly never thought I'd want a woman around all the time, never saw myself with an old lady. But Lily makes me want those things and it took Dr. Graves to make me see that fact. When I first went to see her, I tried the whole denial bull-shit and she quickly put me in my place. I know it won't be easy, but nothing ever worth having is, right?

The women are driving the SUV and us guys are riding our bikes, preferring the freedom that the wind gives us. Whenever we can, we ride. I see Jaxson motion that we're stopping ahead and glance down at my gas gauge. May as well top off my tank and take a piss since we're stopping. Jaxson and Talon pull over to the pumps as well, while the women pull in front of the convenience store and get out. "You doing okay, brother?" Talon asks.

"Yeah, just concerned about Luca and Tig," I admit. All of them, Luca, Tig, Lily, and Ralynn, grew up together and are thicker than thieves. Plus, Luca is Lily's brother thanks to Axe and Cara getting married. I'm fucked in so many ways. Part of me feels like I deserve it for how I handled things, but another part of me wants to scream at all of them that I'm doing the best I can with the hand I've been dealt.

"I expect you'll catch some shit. If you need to, toss it back at them. I get that she's their family and all and I'm not discounting that whatsoever, but at some point, they've all got to realize that neither of you are kids. You're grown ass adults and need to handle any shit on your own," Jaxson adds. I glance at him because if anyone knows about familial interference, it would be him. DJ tried to stick her nose in one time too many and she still can't go to their house unless Hatch is with her to keep her reined in. Although, I'm not sure he's always successful because DJ is a force to be reckoned with.

"Gonna run in and hit the head," I say, eager to finish with this bonding shit. The two of them have been a constant these past few weeks and while I appreciate it tremendously, sometimes, I need my solitude.

"Grab me a water," Talon calls out. I raise my hand to acknowledge I heard him but keep moving. The sooner we finish here, the sooner I reach my Lily.

I'm paying for drinks for all of us, having caught the girls before they could pull out any money when Claree says, "It's going to be okay, Maxum. I have a good feeling about all of this."

"From your mouth to God's ears," I mumble. Not that I hold much belief in an invisible entity; after all, I spent many nights praying and pleading for Him to save me and my mother and He *never* did.

Rae pats my shoulder and states, "Don't take any shit off Uncle Braxton or Luca. It's y'alls life, not theirs. I may not be happy with how you did things and hurt my girl, but I understand more now." Great, fucking great. That means Jaxson's been running his fucking mouth. She sees my look and lowers her voice, saying, "He hasn't said anything to me that you've told him in confidence, Maxum. I'm just good at reading between the lines and I see how you've been working on stuff."

I nod, my shoulders stiff at first, but with her words I feel the tension seeping out. I'm glad my brothers have my back, even though I'm sure they're conflicted as fuck. Dr. Graves telling me to put myself in their shoes has done a world of good when it comes to understanding their reactions. Thankfully, neither Smokey nor Bandit has weighed in because they're too busy dealing with their house full of animals and kids. The only thing that Chief said was that he was willing to listen if I needed him. Law did the same. The brothers all know I'm seeing a therapist; I made that clear at the last church. Hopefully, Dr. Graves can straighten my ass out so I can make Lily mine in all ways.

Because that small spark of hope has blossomed into a constant flame and I feed it daily with everything I recognize is bullshit from my father.

Lily

I'VE CLEANED MY ROOM. TWICE.

Taken a shower.

Changed my sheets, and let me tell you, with one arm in a cast to mid-forearm and the other in a brace, it wasn't easy by a longshot.

Gone through and discarded most of my clothes.

Paced.

Puked.

Brushed my teeth. A-fuckin-gain.

Finally settled on a pair of jeans and a loose pullover t-shirt.

Checked the clock fourteen thousand times. Okay, that's a slight exaggeration.

I'm now down in the common area trying to calm my racing heart. If I wasn't pregnant, I'd be drinking. Unfortunately, that's not an option for the next few months. I make a mental note that I need to find an obstetrician so I can find out how far along I am and make sure everything's okay with the baby.

"Lily, if you don't settle, I'm gonna tie you to a chair," Dad states. He's been sitting there brooding for a few hours now. I heard him and Luca yelling behind the doors of the room they use for church and I suspect that Luca wants to hurt Maxum. Hopefully, Dad won't let him, seeing as he's a brother and he's going to be my baby daddy.

"I'm nervous, Dad," I admit, slumping into the chair across from him. "Y'all weren't there and you didn't hear the tone of voice he used. It'll kill me if he thinks I did this on purpose," I state, waving my hand across my stomach. "I didn't and would never do that to anyone. Dad, I don't think he wants kids," I whisper. That's my biggest fear. I'll live if he decides he doesn't want me; hell, he's already said that once. But if he rejects our child, that will devastate me.

"Well, it's too late for that now, Lily Bug," he says. "Now, what if I go make you a grilled cheese sandwich? You need to eat."

I grin because my dad makes killer grilled cheese. He puts several different types of cheeses together and melts it onto the lightly grilled bread. I hear my stomach start growling and I end up laughing. "I think your grandbaby wants that, Dad," I reply.

"What grandbaby?" I hear a voice, *his* voice, ask. I turn in my seat and see Maxum standing there, a wild-eyed look on his face. "Lily? *What* grandbaby?"

"I think you two kids need to go talk privately," Mom interjects. I shoot her a glare because she was supposed to let me know when he arrived! Her apologetic look has me sighing because knowing her, she got caught up with something else and lost track of time.

"Uh, hey, Maxum." Lame, Lily. Really fucking lame. "You want to follow me? We need to talk." I stand and head to the elevator, grimacing at how I look. They basically gave me an undercut so they could stitch my head and right now, I have my hair pulled up, exposing the bandaged area. I know it's bruised and swollen and because of the stitches, I can't wash my hair. Well, I couldn't do that anyhow because of the fucking cast and the splint, but regardless, I feel disgusting. I wish Cassarah was here; she'd figure out a way to wash my hair.

He doesn't say anything, just follows me into the elevator and I hold back my grin when I see Lucy making a beeline for the open doors. As spoiled as she is, I fear for the day when Luca and Gypsy decide to add to their family with a child. "Which way, Lil?" he asks as we exit the elevator on the second floor of the building. His voice washes over me and I feel my insides clench with need. Fucking hormones. He doesn't want me and even though I'm now carrying his child, I will not force him to be with me.

"I'm down here," I reply, walking toward my room. Lucy stops at Luca's door and I watch in amazement as a small door opens and she walks inside. Fucking hell. They put a doggy door on their bedroom door so she could come and go as she pleases. I unlock my door and step inside. He engages the lock and I barely resist jumping.

"Now that we're away from prying eyes and ears, *what* grandbaby, Lily? Is there something I need to know?" I glance at him and see he's shaking, but it doesn't appear to be from anger. He looks scared shitless and I don't understand why; he's a good man and will be a good daddy.

"I, uh, well, you know that I got hurt last week, right?" At his nod, I continue, "Apparently, since I was unconscious, the doctor had them run a bunch of tests, including a pregnancy test. I don't know how it happened, Maxum, but I'm pregnant." I drop my head and look at my hands, afraid to see the expression on his face.

Silence.

Earth-shattering, profound silence.

After long minutes where it's so quiet I can hear the two of us breathing, I glance at him and my eyes widen. He's now slumped against the floor, his head back, fists clenched and he's shaking so hard he looks like he's having a seizure of some sort. "Maxum? A-a-are you okay?" I whisper. In all the years I've known him, I've seen him in every imaginable situation, but I've never seen him react the way he is right now and I'm scared shitless. I move over to where he's sitting and sit down next to him; not touching, but close enough that he hopefully knows I'm right there.

"I'm gonna fuck this kid up," he quietly states.

"No, you won't," I argue.

"You don't get it, Lil." I can hear the quiver in his voice; this worries me more than his silence ever has.

"Then explain it to me, Maxum." I all but beg him to explain his words to me.

"My mom fled, leaving me behind with a man, my dad, who thought I was nothing more than a mistake and a waste of space. He not only physically abused me, Lil, he also mentally and emotionally destroyed me."

I have a desperate need to touch him, my fingers are literally tingling with the desire to feel his skin, to comfort him, one way or another. My instincts are screaming at me to love him, comfort him, protect him. The pain he's exuding has tears steadily flowing down my face. I reach out and clasp his hand in mine. "Maxum, God, I don't know what to say. I-is that why you… why you kept me at arm's length? I mean, we've been physically intimate, and I consider you one of my best friends, but you've always held something back from me. Is this why?" Every other word I spew comes out in a hiccup. My emotions are already playing havoc on me, but this information he's shared has them raging.

He pulls me on top of him and I'm now straddling him. He wraps me in his arms then moves until his face is buried in my neck. I feel wetness seeping into my skin and realize that this big, strong, vibrantly menacing man is crying. "So sorry, baby, so fucking sorry," he whispers. "I'm fucked up, there's no way I deserve another chance with you. A *real* chance, not just friends with benefits." Jesus, if I wasn't sitting down, his words would've brought me to my knees.

Everything that's happened between us up until now, drastically comes crashing down on me at his words. Is he saying this because he wants *me* or because I'm pregnant with his baby? Despite his recent transgression against me, I love him wholeheartedly – to the depths of my very soul. I know Rae says that maybe he isn't my one, but he is, I feel that down to the marrow of my bones. But I won't stay with him just because of the baby. That's not fair to me, to either of us. "Maxum, I-I don't know what to say here. If it's just because of the baby, then the answer is no." What I really want to do is jump up, scream yes, yes, yes, and claim him whether it's truly what his heart desires or not.

He's *mine*. He's it for me, the only one, there will never be anyone else who does to me, for me, than him. My body desires him, my heart loves him, and my soul needs his for survival.

His voice is low, so low I strain to hear what he says next. "Lily, when I was informed you were hurt, all I could think about was putting my eyes on you to see for myself, to make sure that you are okay. And... I've been seeing a therapist for a few weeks now; she's helping me straighten my head out so I can be the man you deserve. I didn't know about the baby until I got here, sweetheart, so how can you ask that?" The answer to that question has many possibilities.

The need to look into his eyes overcomes me. I lift my head so that I can see his orbs, I want to see if the truth of his words can be seen within their depths. He stares back at me; his eyelashes are still wet from the tears he cried. "Everything's messing with my head right now, Maxum. The concussion, this nasty hair that I can't figure out how to wash, the morning sickness. Are you sure you want all of this in your life?"

He lets out an audible gulp before stating, "Lily, I'm as much of a mess as you, it just doesn't show on the outside, only my attitude. I'll spend the rest of my life proving to you what you mean to me. I-I love you, sweetheart. I know I've got more work to do, and I'm hoping you'll come along for the ride." My heart is pitter-pattering inside of my rib cage… can what he's saying be the truth? I just need to go with it, because if he's willing to fight for us, then so am I. I need to lay it all on the line and show him that love really does exist.

"I love you too, Maxum. But I feel like I need to stay up here for a bit, at least until I'm all healed up. Maybe a little longer, I don't know," I reply. He nods his head, but I can tell he's not terribly happy at the prospect of heading home without me. Time will tell, and I feel like the distance may help put things into perspective… for both of us.

A FEW HOURS LATER WE WAKE UP FROM AN EMOTIONALLY exhausted nap. Honestly, I can't believe we fell asleep, sitting up against the damn wall! I feel so gross and it's making me gag. I can smell myself and feel my gritty, knotted hair. Up until now, it's been sitz baths, and it just hasn't gotten the deed done as far as I'm concerned. I love the way my skin feels after a good soak in the tub, the smell of my hair after a thorough wash and scrub. I miss smelling and feeling like me. "What are you thinking about so loudly?" Maxum startles me from my thoughts.

"Kidnapping you, holding you hostage, never letting you go," I teasingly state.

"That right? You might find that I'm the most accommodating kidnapping victim you'll ever acquire," he jokes back. "Seriously, Lil, tell me what you need. I can see the wheels turning in your head."

"I need to find a way to wash my hair with these stitches and these two useless hands. I can't go two weeks not washing my hair, that's just disgusting," I grouse.

His chuckle makes my heart smile. He reaches out and cups my chin in his hand. "Damn, I've missed the hell out of you, Lily. You've been the one constant thought in my head for weeks now. If you need to stay up here while I get my shit straight, guess I'll be making a lot of trips. I still think I'll be a shitty father, but I'll talk it over with Dr. Graves."

"Handsome, you've got some of the best examples of fatherhood around you at the clubhouse. Not only that, but you know what not to do based on your childhood, right?

Plus, I'll be by your side." I hope he grasps what I'm saying because there's so much love inside him just waiting to burst free.

"Is it okay if I kiss you?" His tone is hesitant sounding and my heart breaks again.

"I think it's a requirement if we're making up," I reply, grinning at him. As his lips lower to claim mine in a soft kiss, I realize I'm finally home.

10

MAXUM

For several hours we sit there, curled in each other's arms, but I know I'm still feeling exhausted from the lack of sleep I've had from the few weeks she's been away. I'm sure Axe and Luca are waiting to jump down my throat; only right now, I've got a beautiful but hurt woman in my arms who needs rest. "C'mon, baby, let's get more comfortable," I whisper.

She nods and I help her stand up before I do the same. "I… uh… I need to hit the bathroom first," she states, blushing. I chuckle because during the course of our friendship, I've been with her when her headaches were so bad, she was throwing up and I held her hair back. It's gotta be a woman thing to get embarrassed about something that's a natural part of life. Shrugging, I take off my boots and cut and lay on top of the bed, before grabbing the blanket she has on the bottom. My woman loves her fuzzy blankets, that's for damn sure. When she joins me, I pull her into my arms and lay a kiss on her forehead. I'm so wiped, that even though she's finally back where she belongs and I realize that fact, I don't get hard.

"Love you, Lily. Let's get some rest and then I'll see if I can figure out how to wash your hair."

"For that alone, I'll love you forever," she mumbles sleepily.

I'm still smiling as I drift off to sleep.

I DON'T KNOW WHAT WAKES ME UP, BUT OPENING MY EYES, I notice Cara just inside the door frame. I know I locked it; my mind is wondering how the hell did she get inside? Not wanting to wake Lily, I give her a look and she quietly says, "Luca has a key. I wanted to check on the two of you because you've been up here for a few hours. Go back to sleep; I'll keep Braxton and Luca away until you're ready." I smile and nod before curling back into Lily. I eventually fall back into slumber and it's the best sleep I've had since we split up.

"A GARBAGE BAG? REALLY, MAXUM?" SHE ASKS, LOOKING at me then the bag I'm holding.

"I called Cassarah to see how I could best wash your hair, baby. The main thing is to keep it dry, so I've got some waterproof bandages for that, but you can't get your cast wet either. Thus, the garbage bags."

She rolls her eyes at me and I lean down and kiss her, before I proceed to get her ready to get into the shower.

Lily

THERE'S SOMETHING SO INTIMATE ABOUT ANOTHER PERSON taking the time and energy to bathe you, y'know? I mean, we've had some showers together in the past that were raw and downright dirty, but right now, it's not about that. He's almost reverent, for lack of a better word, about how he's touching me and making sure I'm clean. He has washed my hair twice so that I don't feel like it's disgusting and dingy anymore. Since one arm is in a cast, the other is splinted, I've had to rely on others to assist me. Having your dad wash you like you were still a child is humiliating… but I took what I could. Right now, though, I'm in absolute heaven. Of course, my damn hormones are all over the place because I nearly break down in tears when he's shaving my legs. As he leans in and kisses my stomach, he says, "I'm going to be better than my father was, peanut." The sincerity in his voice makes my heart sing; I've always known he was the one for me and he's finally gotten with the program. I'm soaring in relief and rub my hand over his head as he has a conversation with our unborn child. Witnessing him overcoming the trauma of his past, seeing the love shine in his eyes, it's awe-inspiring and I'm grateful to be part of his healing.

Once we're done, he gets me fully dried and then helps dress me. While I want him, hell, I always want him, right now I'm enjoying this closeness that has nothing to do with sex. "Ready to grab something to eat?" he asks.

"And face the proverbial music? Sure, I've been looking forward to this since I knew you were coming up," I reply. I may be a bit snarky, though, because he chuckles then leans in and kisses my forehead. It gives me the tingles every single time his lips touch me, but I wish he'd plant those lips on mine. But beggars can't be choosers and all of that shit, so I'll take what he's willing to give.

"It's gonna be fine, baby. You'll see," he states. I'm glad he's so fucking confident. Every time Gypsy or Mom mention the baby and what needs to be done, Luca positively glowers. Dad isn't much better, but I know that he's excited about his first grandchild. Knowing Dad the way I do, he just wishes things had happened in a different way. I know this is bringing back memories of the past for him, so I'm being patient every time he mutters something into thin air. Luca, well, he's always been my protector in every sense of the word. When I cry he holds me, when I'm angry he beats someone up. That's the way it's always been; he and Tig were always watching out for us girls. The thing I can say about my family is that they may not always do things the way we want them to, but every action and word to us, and for us, is done with love.

"I hope you're right, Maxum. I get that my 'position' in the club makes everyone feel like they've got a say-so in my life, but dammit, this doesn't concern any of them. The brothers wouldn't interfere with you if it wasn't me." I know I'm right about this because I've seen it happen over the years. The dance that Jaxson did regarding Ralynn. Talon and Claree and their situation. Hell, no one so much as batted an eye when Luca came home with Gypsy and her dog, for fuck's sake! So, they need to cut us some fucking slack. There's a pattern here, and it needs to be broken. Just because I have a vagina and not a dick doesn't mean I don't deserve the same treatment.

"First you're snarky, now you're feisty. Kind of liking this side of you, Lily," he says. Leaning up, I nip his ear causing his eyes to glaze over with lust before he tampers it down.

"You ain't seen nothing yet," I caution. "I'm also overly emotional, cry at the drop of a hat, and when I'm not sick, I'm eating everything that's not nailed down. Hell, I even ate mushrooms the other night," I reply.

"Who are you and what have you done with my Lily?" he teases. "Because my Lily hates mushrooms even though I don't think she's ever tasted them." This is true, I hate the thought of even placing one in my mouth. Usually, I'd be gagging if I saw anyone eating them. They look funny and smell atrocious. Well, that's my opinion of them anyway.

"Maxum, they're gross! I hate the texture." At my outburst, he starts laughing and pulls me in for a hug.

"God, woman, I love the hell out of you. C'mon, let's head downstairs and see what they've all gotta say."

Maxum

I'M PUTTING ON A GOOD FRONT FOR HER, BUT FUCK, I'M nervous. All of my brothers know I'm seeing a therapist, but I feel like Luca and Tig will both have shit to say to me. Just hoping I can keep my cool facade going, because where my relationship with her is concerned, it's none of their fucking business. I won't lie either about the struggles I've faced and am still facing. The time for me keeping that shit buried deep down is dead and gone. I hear a noise and then hear her giggles. Looking down, I see Gypsy's dog, Lucy, prancing alongside of us. Today, for some possessed reason, she has on one of those doggy sweaters. "They *dress* her?" I ask.

"Not all the time, but it's starting to get cooler and Luca was worried she was cold, so he hit the pet store and bought her an entire wardrobe." She's now laughing hysterically as she tells me that because they apparently get snow up here, he also found doggy boots or some shit. I've seen a lot in my days, but I've never seen anything like how they treat this dog. She follows us into the elevator and before I can push the button, she does so, causing me to shake my head again. They say dogs are smart but I've never had one so I've never witnessed anything like I have since meeting Lucy. She's a phenomenon to me, one I'm considering for myself.

"Ah, there you two are," Cara says as we step off the elevator and into the common room. "We've got breakfast set out in the kitchen, y'all come and eat." Yeah, we never managed to come back down last night and right now, my stomach is reminding me that it likes eating.

Keeping my arm around Lily's waist since I can't quite hold her hand right now, we walk into the kitchen where everyone else is sitting at the huge-ass table eating. "Morning, brother," Axe says, looking at me. Good, he doesn't look like he's about to take me out back and kill me so I'll count it as a win. "Morning, sweetheart. How's your head today?"

"Better, Dad. Plus, I'm clean!" she replies, doing a little twirl. "I mean, it still hurts, but I don't want to take my meds until I see a doctor because I don't want to hurt the baby."

"Are we seriously going to just sit here, pretend like nothing's happened and ignore the elephant in the room?" Luca questions. I sigh because it was too good to be true.

"Luca," Axe growls. "Now is not the time or place for you to start shit. Besides, like I've already said, it's not your business."

"Like fuck it's not! She's my sister, Dad." I've never seen Luca so angry or speak to his dad like he is.

"And, he is one of your brothers, Luca. Loyalty, respect, honor… or have you forgotten the code we stand by? It's her life, no one interfered in yours. Y'know, your sister doesn't need the additional stress of anyone arguing; it's one of her headache triggers."

Luca's shoulders slump a little before he glares at me. "You and I are gonna have words, brother," he states.

"Wouldn't expect anything less from her brother, Luca," I admit.

"Gypsy, Lucy's sweater today is so cute," Lily interjects. I give her a smile at her obvious subject change.

Gypsy laughs and points at Luca. "Blame it on her daddy."

"What? I can't make sure our girl stays warm?" Luca asks. "Y'all fix your plates before it gets cold. Or eaten. Of course, Lily seems to have us all beat in that department lately."

I watch her face turn red at his words referencing her appetite. I noticed during our shower the tiniest baby bump and realize that I can't wait until she's swollen with our baby and needs me to take care of her like I did today. Maybe other men don't do that for their women, but for me, taking care of Lily has never been an issue, even when I wasn't letting my heart get fully involved.

After breakfast, Luca motions me into the room where they do church. I don't miss the fact that Tig, Jaxson, and Talon follow closely behind. The only one not here is Maddox, but he's apparently out on a job site already. Once we're seated, I take a deep breath and remind myself that I'm becoming a new person thanks to Dr. Graves.

The door shuts and Luca takes his place at the head of the table. "Dad may say this is none of my business, but I beg to differ. Lily has always been mine to protect, and I've let her down where it comes to you. I'm not okay with how this has played out. I wanna know, how are you going to fix this and what are your plans regarding my sister and niece or nephew?" Right to the point, Luca's never been one to play cat and mouse games.

"Luca, no disrespect intended, but don't you think that's between Lily and me?" I'm trying really hard to remember he's my club brother.

"No, I really don't. You see, Maxum, I'm her family. You may be my brother, but right now, you're the man who's hurt my sister and that doesn't sit well with me." Jaxson shakes his head and Talon gives Luca a glare. Tig, however, looks ready for a brawl and the excitement shining in his eyes pisses me off.

"I'm seeking help, Luca. I've been seeing a counselor to deal with what happened to me and she's helping me to rewire the way things cycle through my head. We're rewiring it so to speak. Bad things happened to me growing up, things I'm just now able to share and talk about."

"We've all had bad things happen to us as kids, Maxum, but I never treated Gypsy like a second-class citizen," Luca growls.

"I'm sorry that you see things that way, Luca. But we'll never move forward from here if you're not letting me share my past and help me build my future. We're family too, Luca, in case you've forgotten." My irritation with him is seeping out with my words and the tone leaving my vocal cords. If he wants a fight, I'm willing to give him one, though I doubt Axe will be happy with that outcome.

11

LILY

When the guys all headed into the room and closed the door, I wanted to stomp my feet and throw a temper tantrum. How dare they interfere in my life! I've always been there for them to talk to without putting my fat nose into their business.

"Lily, you need to let them hash this out on their own," Dad advises me.

"Your dad's right, Lily. They won't be able to let it rest or move on until they do. The best thing for you to do is concentrate on building your relationship with Maxum since y'all have a baby on the way. They'll talk it out, deal with it, and keep on trucking like nothing ever happened," Mom says as she takes all of the dishes and places them in the dishwasher.

"We're starting to get into a good place, I don't want them to push him away." I sulk like a sullen child. "No offense to anyone, but this is about us, not anyone else. Everyone needs to mind their p's and q's and let us deal with our situation the way we see fit."

Dad sighs as he runs his fingers through his beard. "Lily, what part of family don't you understand? We meddle with the best of intentions. Honestly? I'm trying really hard here not to go all Neanderthal and pull the Dad card. I'm being patient, understanding, and am *not* beating that man's ass for knocking my unmarried daughter up with my grandchild. Give us some time and patience as we figure out the new roles we are playing in your life."

"Honey, your dad and Luca are used to being the only men in your life. They've always felt responsible for your well-being and ensuring your happiness. Step back, look at things from the other end of the spectrum. One day, this will be you and Maxum, how will you deal with that when the day comes?" Mom, always the voice of reason, pipes in to ask.

I think about her words for a few minutes. Sighing, I finally say, "I guess you're right, it's just that no one really butted their noses into anyone else's relationship. I don't think it's fair that just because I'm your daughter and Luca's sister that Maxum has to face the proverbial firing squad."

"And once they hash shit out, they'll step back, I'll make sure of it," Dad vows. "Our guys all know he's seeing a therapist, but Luca and Tig have no idea what he's dealt with in his past. I'm glad that Jaxson and Talon made the trip, because they've been beside him since he started. Hatch too, and the only reason he didn't come is because he and DJ are watching the kids. Plus, DJ is somewhat of a wild card right now. She keeps bouncing between it being none of anyone's business to wanting to hit him for hurting you, so it's best that she stayed home. You have a lot of people who love you, Lily. They've watched you grow up, been with you all these years during your trips to the hospital or being down for days with a headache. It may not be their business, per se, but for all of them, they've been such a big part of your life, they feel like they should have a say-so, even if they really don't."

"I just don't want to cause an issue between the brothers, Dad," I admit. "I won't give him up, but I also won't have him constantly feeling like he's under the gun. That's not fair and it's not right. You need to use your president's voice and tell them all to grow the fuck up, stop acting like a bunch of nattering hens, and let us work through it with his therapist."

Dad starts laughing. "Nattering hens? I swear, Lily, that I never know what's gonna come out of your mouth."

"Higher education does that for a person," Mom replies, leaning down to kiss Dad. I turn my head when the kiss gets heated, not wanting to see their obvious display of affection. Growing up around the two of them was...interesting, to say the least. Before Nan moved out, we often found ourselves being taken to the park or out for an ice cream so that the two of them could have some 'alone' time. Then, when Nan moved out, they started taking long naps on the weekends! Usually, though, they'd grab a movie that we wanted to watch, all the junk food we asked for, and pizza. Luca and I finally figured out what was going on after we went through health class, a fact that still embarrasses me. I mean, they're not ancient by a longshot, but no one wants to think of their parents having sex and the fact that they went on to have my younger brother and sister is mind-blowing.

"So, on a scale of one to ten, how are you really feeling?" Mom asks, after plopping down on Dad's lap.

"Emotionally, I'm at the stratosphere. I know we've still got shit to work through, and he's worried about being a good parent, but I reminded him he's got some great examples in his own brothers, plus I'm going to be there as well. Physically, I'm still exhausted, even though we slept yesterday and last night away, for the most part. My headache is still there but like I said, I don't want to take my meds until I see a doctor to make sure it won't hurt the baby. My stitches itch and so does my casted wrist."

Mom gives me a concerned look. "How bad's the head, Lily?"

"Pretty bad," I admit. "I took some Tylenol, but I'm nauseous. Only I don't know if it's from the concussion, a 'normal' headache, or morning sickness."

"Maybe you need to lay down, then," she replies. "I had wanted to take you, Claree, Gypsy, Maysen, and Rae shopping, but we can do that later or even tomorrow."

"I'm not going anywhere until they're done with their meeting," I retort, crossing my arms over my ample chest. I know I probably look as intimidating as a gnat, especially since I'm petite and both arms are fucked up, but I'm trying to get my point across.

"It's club…" Dad starts to say.

"It's *not* fucking club business, Dad," I rebut. "It's my brother showing his damn ass and barking his authority, pissing on his territory, so to speak. Sorry, Gypsy." I glance apologetically at her as she comes back into the kitchen.

"Girl, don't apologize. I know how *intense* Luca can get. Trust me. Lucy is a prime example." She waves her hand at the little dog who followed her into the kitchen and is now at her bowl eating her breakfast.

I start giggling because he has started a like page for Lucy on social media and posts pictures and what-not of her. Hell, she's got more followers than I've got friends. How is that even possible? "As over the top as he is with her, how will he be when y'all have kids?" I muse.

She rolls her eyes before slumping in the chair. "I suspect I'll be allowed to lift nothing heavier than a cotton ball and that's if he allows me to even get out of the damn bed." At her words, both Mom and Dad start to chuckle.

"Oh, honey, you're just seeing the tip of the iceberg when it comes to how protective he is over those he loves," Mom says.

We all sit and chat for a little longer. The more time passes, the more anxious and worried I become. What in the hell is taking those guys so long?

Maxum

I LAY IT ALL OUT ON THE TABLE FOR MY BROTHERS. THERE are things I'm sharing that even Talon and Jaxson aren't aware of. My past is not pretty, and now, they all know all of my deepest darkest secrets.

"Your mom just abandoned you and left you alone with that piece of shit?" Tig questions, anger evident on his face. I'm thankful that he's feeling this deep, but I know him, and he allows his anger to override his common sense sometimes.

"She did," I acknowledge.

"Where's your dad now?" Luca asks. I can see a plan forming in his mind, and it worries me. He and Tig together, when pissed, can form an avalanche of epic proportions. Mother Nature doesn't have shit on these two.

"Guys, seriously, whatever's going through your heads, let it go. I'm getting the help I need, and I'm ready to let the past go. I need y'all to just breathe and have my back. Don't go all rogue and search out my parents to dole out justice as you see fit." Both of them look at me as if I've lost my mind for not letting them seek out some revenge on my behalf.

"We at least need to track the two of them down and make sure that you, Lily and y'alls baby will be safe," Jaxson pipes in.

"I agree, Maxum. At least let Bandit do his thing and see if he can find out where they've slithered off to. A snake may shed its skin, but it can be just as lethal in its new sheath."

"I understand where you all are coming from, but I don't want to wake the beast if he's still sleeping and has forgotten all about me. My biggest fear is reminding him of my existence so he can play his methodical games with my mind and body. He can't physically hurt me anymore; I'd fight him back now that I'm older, but he has the ability to rock my world if he comes back around. I have Lily and our baby to think of now. Not only that, but he can and would hurt anyone who's important to me, and with y'all being my brothers, that means your old ladies and kids. I can't let anything from my past touch even a hair on either of their heads, or risk any of y'alls," I implore.

"It would be the worst mistake of either your sperm donor's or egg carrier's lives, if they ever came back just to fuck with our family." Luca lets out a menacing growl. I hide my grin because we may not be that type of club, but most of us have a military background and aren't afraid to throw down if necessary. I just don't want my brothers putting themselves in the line of fire, especially if my bastard of a father has forgotten about me.

"Oh, we'd open a can of whoop ass on them," Tig states, while punching his fist into his hand. "It's been a bit since I've had a good brawl."

"Jesus," I mutter under my breath. "You two are just as crazy as fucking Bandit and Smokey."

"I object to that statement. They're the class clowns, while we are badasses, not comic relief," Tig proclaims profusely.

"I disagree, Maxum," Talon interjects. "Tig is Bandit and Smokey rolled into one and Luca is a mixture of Hatch and Axe." I find this hysterical given the fact that Tig is Twisted's son. Maybe he spent too much time with Smokey and Bandit when he was little because now that Talon mentions it...

"I never thought about it that way," Jaxson states, running his fingers through his beard.

"Okay, back to business. Are we good, Luca?" I ask. When we leave this room, I want us back to how we were before.

"We're good, brother. Just keep in mind, that I won't always stay out of things. Seeing Lily hurt or upset sets off my protective side. I can't help it; it's always been that way and always will be." He unapologetically shrugs his shoulders.

"I get it, Luca," I say. "You're a great brother to Lily. I'm happy that she has a loving, caring family. It's something I'm learning to accept for myself. No one here gave birth to me, but sometimes family doesn't share the same blood."

"Unfortunately, sometimes life isn't fair. We can't help who we're born to, but we can choose the family we want when we're older. Sharing the same bloodline doesn't mean those people are right for us. Finding where we belong and being accepted for who we are is what matters. Love, loyalty, honor and respect, brother, that's what we have for you," Luca implores. I can feel his words crack down that last chunk of wall that I put in place to protect myself.

"Thank you, brother," I say.

The four of us walk over to each other, shake hands, and do the man hug, slap thing. All is good, and I'm relieved that this is behind us.

"Let's gather the men, go for a ride, and hit the pub. I'm starving," Luca says rubbing his stomach.

"Hey! Why not go to my bar? We have food, drinks and shit," Tig offensively asks.

"Fine, you tit bag, we'll go to the damn bar," Luca states. Tig looks like a kid in the candy store who just got his favorite treat. He's literally bouncing on the balls of his feet in excitement. If he starts clapping his hands, I'm having him committed for observation and treatment.

12

LILY

It's been two weeks since Maxum had to leave me and head home. I'm beginning to think I've made a horrible mistake staying behind. I've cried myself to sleep several nights, missing the way he holds me, wrapped up in the tight embrace of his arms as I fall asleep each and every night. Not a day has gone by that we haven't spoken on the phone, but his voice makes my libido go crazy since my hormones are spiked. I'm almost to the point of begging him to have phone sex during a video chat so I can get some relief.

"Lily, you seem miserable since your parents and Maxum went home. Are you sure being here is the best thing for you?" Gypsy asks.

"I stayed here because I thought seeing the doctors who treated me from day one was the best course of action. I didn't realize I'd be so damn sad, or I may have made a different choice," I admit to her.

"Lily Bug, you can have your files transferred from a doctor here to yours back home. It's not that hard to find an orthopedist; believe it or not they reside in every city and state," Luca, the eternal wiseass says as he sits next to us, taking a big gulp of coffee.

"Well, aren't you just wise beyond your years," I snarkily state.

He taps his fingers to his head, he's always ready and prepared to come back with a smartass response. "I've always been the brains in our operation, Lily. You've always known this, why are you acting so surprised now?"

"God! You drive me insane sometimes," I state in a pissy tone.

"That's what brothers are for," he quips.

"Fuck off, Luca!" I shout out my annoyance.

"Come on, Gypsy. You heard my sister; she gave us a direct order." He stands up, grabs her hand and pulls her from her chair.

"Oh, and the big bad biker president has to do as his little sister proclaims," Gypsy teases him while winking in my direction.

"In this instance, yes. Absofuckinglutely." He steadily pulls her from the room as she giggles.

"Yeah, sure. Leave me here alone, I'm not sad or lonely or anything… go have fun!" I shout out to the now empty room. Deciding enough is enough, I head up to my room, pack the meager belongings I have with me, write a note for Luca and Gypsy, then hit the road. I'll call my doctors here when I get home and have all of my files transferred… it's time to go back where I belong. To Maxum, to my parents, aunts and uncles, and the twins. I've missed them all so damn much. As I think about this, I begin to cry. When are these damn hormones gonna give my swollen puffy eyes a break?

I've been traveling for two hours when my bladder can't take it anymore. I pull into a nondescript gas station, the only one within a twenty-mile radius according to my GPS. Shit, I hate these small mom-and-pop owned stations, I like the bigger chains where there's more people. They're better maintained and I like the safety in numbers thing. Since I'm a single female traveling alone, the feeling of dread washes over me every time I have to stop at a place like this.

If one of these stations were in my hometown, I'd feel more secure, but being in a town I know nothing about freaks me the hell out. My imagination is always playing tricks on my mind. Someone's following me, watching my every move, the hills have eyes… yada, yada, yada.

I quickly rush in, find the restroom, do my business and hit the car again. Once I'm safely back inside the confinement of my vehicle, I lather up my hands in sanitizer and breathe a breath of relief. I turn my map back on to lead me home. I can't wait to sleep in the comfort of my own bed again. It also won't hurt to have Maxum by my side each and every night.

A few hours later, I pull into town and press the button on my steering wheel. "Call Maxum," I instruct it.

"Calling Jaxson," the voice responds.

"No, call Maxum," I order.

"Calling Maddox," the annoying bitch says.

"Fucking hell," I cry out.

"Calling Luca," it says as the stupid bitch dials and I hear the ringing through my speakers.

"Miss me already?" I can't help it, I burst out into laughter. "Lily, are you having a mental breakdown? Where are you, are you okay?" The worry in his voice should settle me down, instead it has the opposite effect. "Gypsy, I think Lily has lost her mind, pack our bags we're going to find her and make sure she's safe."

I can hear Gypsy in the background, the sound of her concerned voice snaps me out of it. "I'm fine, Luca. I asked the car to call Maxum, she named every male in my directory before I shouted out fucking hell and she dialed you." This time, all three of us laugh. I can't help it, it's hysterical.

"Are you home?" Luca settles down and asks me.

"Pulling into town now, it's why I wanted to call Maxum," I inform him.

"Hands free isn't all it's cracked up to be when you try and call your lover and instead get your brother." Gypsy laughs in the background. I now realize Luca placed me on speaker.

"Don't say lover to my sister! It's gross, I need to cleanse my ears now, woman. It's just wrong to use that word when it comes to her," I hear Luca growl and Gypsy squeak in the background.

"Okay! There's only so much a sister should hear and see. I'll talk to you two later." I quickly disconnect, knowing where that playful banter was heading. I shiver as disgust rolls through me, yuck!

Maxum

My face lights up when I grab my phone and see that Lily's calling. "Hey, beautiful," I quickly answer.

"So, I was thinking Chinese or pizza for dinner, which would you prefer?" I'm a bit dazed and confused by the question.

"I can't make it tonight, Lil. I won't even get out of the shop until six or seven tonight." I disappointingly sigh into the receiver.

"Well, that bites. I just pulled up to my apartment and it looks awfully lonely. I was thinking of an early night in with you."

"Could you repeat that?" I quickly stand up, dropping the wrench from my hand.

"I'm home, Maxum. I couldn't spend another day without you. I've missed you so much," she hiccups into the phone. I can tell she's crying and it breaks a part of me.

I must be wearing a pained expression on my face because Jaxson quickly abandons his work and rushes over to me. "What is it?"

I place my hand over the speaker and say, "Lil's home, she's crying man."

"Then you need to get over to her. I've got things covered here, we're not far enough behind that you need to sacrifice some time with your old lady. Get going." He points his finger toward my bike.

"I'm coming, Lily. I'll be there in ten," I gleefully announce.

"It's been too long since I've seen you, Maxum. Hurry that fine ass up and get home." Home, she is my home, it makes me ecstatic to realize that fact. I'll get to experience her, and this euphoric feeling I feel when she's near, for the rest of my life.

"Lil, we just saw each other four days ago." I went up to see her for a quick weekend reprieve from the shop. I also needed to lay eyes and hands on her.

"It feels like an eternity," she whispers.

"I'll agree to that. Let me get off, baby, so I can come home," I say, even though the last thing I want to do is let her off.

"Home," she whispers.

"Home," I repeat.

"I like the sound of that, Maxum."

"Me too, Lil, me too."

13

MAXUM

Lil has been home for two months now, and today, we get to see the baby. Her ultrasound appointment has the family making bets. The pot is up to a thousand dollars, all of which is being donated to the home I've been looking at. I want to surprise Lily and give us a house to bring our baby home to. I pray that she's not disappointed that she didn't get to hunt with me for the perfect place to call ours. But, I hope that the gesture alone rebukes any ill-will she'll hold over me and realize that this is me, telling her that I'm here to stay. Permanently.

"Do you want to know what it is?" I ask her as we walk hand in hand into the doctor's office.

"It's a baby, Maxum," she giggles.

"I know that, smartass. I mean, are we wanting to know if it's a boy or a girl?" I reach over and tickle her side, she squeaks out a laugh causing me to chuckle in response.

"If you don't stop, I'm going to pee myself! The baby's on my bladder today, apparently."

I grin because it seems like every five minutes, she's running to the bathroom and I suspect that the bigger she gets, the worse it's going to be. "Baby, you saying you need some of those adult diapers?" I tease. She pokes me and I lean in and kiss her.

She gives me a look and I know she's got something else on her mind. I wait and sure enough, she starts talking. "I think we should do one of those gender reveal parties that everyone is doing these days. Our family can be surrounding us as we hear the results of what we're having together. It would mean a lot to them," she worriedly states. I guess she's worried about how I'll respond to this news. I think it's a great idea which I tell her. "You wouldn't be disappointed? It could take a few weeks to get everything put together and find out."

"Anticipation would make it that much sweeter when we hear," I inform her.

"And drive us crazy in the meantime," she states.

"This may be true, but I love a surprise. Plus, the thought of everyone being included in finding out has an appeal to me. I can be patient," I tell her.

"Ugh, it's never been one of my strong points," she reminds me.

We make it up to the counter and sign her in. As soon as our butts hit the seat, a nurse comes out calling Lily back. "Hey, Lily, let's get your weight before we head into the exam room."

"I have to use a rubber band to keep my jeans up, I'm not sure if I wanna hear and see how much weight I've gained," she begrudgingly says.

"You're growing a little person, Lil. If you weren't gaining weight, that'd mean something's wrong with our baby." I try to appease her. I can see the pounds she's added since becoming pregnant, but she's one of those women whose weight gain is mostly carried in her stomach region. It's like a little basketball is inflating inside of her… it's cute as fuck if you ask me. It's perfectly rounding with our baby's growth, her tits and ass have enlarged, but I'll never voice that to her. She'd likely cut off my balls and hang them up on her rearview mirror.

The nurse jots the information down, then has her sit while she takes her blood pressure and other vitals. Once she's done, she leads us into an exam room and asks, "Y'all are getting the ultrasound today, correct? Are you hoping to find out the baby's sex?"

"Well, yes and no," Lily replies. "We want to know but not know, if that makes sense." The nurse looks puzzled, so Lily continues in a rush, "We want to do a gender reveal party for our family and find out at the same time they do." At her explanation, the nurse's brow unfurrows and she smiles.

"Ah, gotcha. I'll make sure the tech prints it off and places it in a sealed envelope. I presume you have someone making a cake?"

"I, uh, I haven't figured that part out yet," Lily admits.

"Well, you're in luck. There's a fantastic baker in town here and she does gender reveal cakes. Having tasted them, I can promise, you won't be disappointed. If you're interested, I'll get you one of her cards."

I speak up and say, "Please get us the card. And thank you

for letting us know. It's our first baby, so we're a bit clueless about things."

"I'll bring it back in a few minutes, then. Lily, can you go ahead and get comfortable and pull your shirt up and slide your pants down a little bit? I'll cover you with this wonderful paper blanket," the nurse states, causing Lily to giggle again. I like this look on her; she's still getting headaches and even though the doctor found a medicine she can take that won't hurt the baby, she's so fucking stubborn that she has to be past the point of no return before she'll take it. I make a mental note to mention that to the doctor so she can reassure my woman.

"Lil?"

"Yeah," she responds.

"I sorta had a different idea come to mind when we talked about the gender reveal thing," I hesitantly say because she may not like my idea at all.

"Okay, tell me about it while I put on this paper gown, it's thin as hell; you'll have to tell me if it's see through or not." I laugh at her words, then quickly assure her with a nod that I'd comply with her wishes.

"So, this was my thought. I'm a biker, your family are all bikers and our little one needs a cut… right?"

"Yes, Maxum, our baby will have a cut just like all the little ones that have come into the family before ours." She chuckles. "Tell me about your idea, honey."

"When you told me what you'd like to do, my first thought was us opening up a box with either a pink or blue cut for our little one."

"Oh, Maxum! I adore that idea. Let's go with that!"

Lily

My excitement is running like hot lava through my veins. I can't help but picture Maxum and I tearing into a box together to discover if we're having a little girl or a little boy. I'm so happy he's come up with the idea he has, but I need to entrust someone to keep our secret and have the cut made for us. My mind wanders over who it should be. Rae is my best friend, but like her mother, she can't keep a secret to save her life. I want my mother to be surprised that day like we will be. As I go through the list of people in the club, it dawns on me that Claree is the perfect choice.

"I'm going to set up a lunch with me and Claree and have

her take care of the gender reveal party, that way our moms only have to worry over decorating the clubhouse and plan the meals," I inform Maxum.

"What are we gonna tell the nurse about the cake?" He's so damn sweet, always worrying over hurting someone's feelings.

"We can still do the cake, just not cut into it until after we've opened the package. I think it would be so much fun!" I answer.

There's a knock on the door as Maxum hurries up and covers my lower area with the blanket while I get situated on the exam table. "Come in," he hollers out.

"Hello, Lily and Maxum," Dr. Sandoval says as she saunters into the room. She's a sweet woman in her late forties and she's been nice to both of us. She doesn't look down her nose at my man for his attire like most snot-nosed people do.

"Hi, Doc," I answer back with a smile on my face.

"Are we excited today to see the baby?" she asks, and I'm surprised that she seems just as eager as we are.

"Been counting down the days, Doc," Maxum answers before I have the chance to.

"Okay, we're going to listen to the baby's heartbeat, get

some measurements, and head on over to the ultrasound room," she informs us.

"Sounds like a plan," I gleefully say.

WE JUST FINISHED WITH THE EXAM, TALKED ABOUT MY headaches, and other important information was shared on what I can expect for the next couple of weeks. It's amazing how quickly things can form for a baby who's still nestled deeply inside of me. I'm happy to hear that I can still get my next round of hormones inserted into my hip to help keep my migraines at a minimum. Between the Bio-TE treatments, my vitamins, plus my regular regime of meds, I'm experiencing more energy than I've had in years and I'm loving life.

Dr. Sandoval leads us down the hall and escorts us into the room. There's a bed, a sofa, a chair next to the bed, and a huge television hung up on the wall. "We like our patients, their spouses, and anyone else they bring with them to not only be comfortable, but also get to see the baby well," she explains.

"It's a marvelous set up," I say to her.

"Okay, I'm gonna go find Marla, our tech, and we'll be back in shortly. You can keep your clothes on, just pull your shirt up under your breasts and pull your pants down to your hips. I can't wait to see the little one and double-check on our measurements."

Once she walks out the door, I quickly get myself settled on the bed, get my clothes situated as she asked, and Maxum sits in the chair next to me, holding my hand. I can feel his fingers twitching and his hand is sweating. "Maxum, are you okay?"

"I'm nervous, excited and a whole handful of emotions all rolled up into one right now," he answers, and his eyes meet mine. They're wide and I can see fear laced in them.

"Maxum, this is our new beginning. This baby is going to help make us better people. We've got this, baby. We can do anything as long as we're together," I reassure him.

"You're right. Love you, Lil."

"Love you back," I lovingly say.

"Knock, knock," Dr. Sandoval says as she enters the room followed by a mousy woman who I'm assuming is Marla.

"Good, you're ready," Dr. Sandoval says, then she introduces us to Marla. Once Marla begins setting up the machine, she comes to life and I am immediately put at ease by her.

"Let's see this baby," Marla says with a smile laced on her face. I can tell that she really loves her job.

She puts some gel on my stomach then places a wand over my skin. It's nice and warm since they keep it in a warmer. The screen comes to life with a whooshing sound and I see our baby in real time as he or she is sucking on their thumb. "Oh hell, our baby's gonna be a binky sucker," Maxum says in a huff.

"You'll come to rely on that pacifier when nothing is comforting that baby," Dr. Sandoval chuckles.

Marla goes on to show us the fingers, toes, ribs, as she takes measurements of the baby's arms, legs, etc. I'm so enthralled with watching our baby, that I don't pay much attention to all of the details. Maxum, however, has honed in on every word they are saying, all the while, never taking his eyes from where our baby is being shown.

14

LILY

As we walk out of the building, I'm looking down at the sonogram pictures while Maxum leads me to our vehicle. We're so happy and I can't wait to share these photos with the world. "Let's go home and celebrate," Maxum says.

"What'cha have in mind?" I question.

“A little of this, a little of that, none of which requires clothing.” The butterflies begin to fly in my stomach as they always do when the prospect of having sexy time with my man gets brought up.

“Naked house day?” I ask, waggling my eyebrows at him.

“You took the words right out of my mouth, baby,” he says as he leans down and captures my lips with his own. “Come on, Lil, I can’t wait much longer to be buried deep inside of you.”

Needless to say, it only took fifteen minutes to make it home instead of the normal twenty. Five minutes shaved off of our drive time, means more make-out time for me. When he pulls in the driveway to my place, I hurriedly unbuckle. I kind of hope he’s up for a bath because even with the cloth they gave me to wipe that gel off, I still feel sticky as hell and that’s not sexy to me! I start to open my door and he growls at me. “You know better, Lil.”

“Maxum, I’m just anxious,” I admit. “Plus, I want to get cleaned up and get this gel off of me.” And I *am* nervous. We’ve slept next to each other since I got home, but other than some hot and heavy make-out sessions, we’ve been sex free. Not by our choice, however. No, when I first came back, Maxum took me to his next appointment with Dr. Graves. It was her suggestion that even though we were pregnant and knew each other pretty well, at least intimately, that we focus on building an impenetrable foundation. So, every week, for the past two months, we've had homework assignments that ranged from silly to scary to serious. Yesterday, at our appointment, she smiled and said that she felt we were ready to resume 'all aspects of a normal, loving relationship' and when Maxum pressed, she said we could reintroduce sex into our lives. I wanted to last night, but the baby had other ideas and I had heartburn from dinner. Definitely not sexy when you're burping every other minute, so I had to beg off. I smile thinking about how Maxum ran out in the middle of the night to track down some more ginger ale since that's the only thing that really helps. God, I love this man beyond words!

Today, though, it's a whole different story and my biggest worry is the fact that my body has changed so fucking much. Maxum hasn't said anything, but I know he can see the beach ball I've got underneath my shirt. And *why* didn't anyone tell me that my tits and ass were going to grow exponentially as well? I make a mental note to have a discussion with my girls because they should've told me! I'm scared that he's going to take one look at my fat, naked self and run screaming from the bedroom. I'm so deep in my thoughts that I miss him getting out of the truck then coming over to my side until he gently turns my head to look at him. "Lily? Whatever's going on in that head of yours that has you looking like a cross between someone who has constipation and someone who just scratched off the winning lottery ticket, just stop. It's me, baby, and you, remember? No matter what?" I nod and he unbuckles me and helps me out, not letting go of my hand as we walk to the door.

Once it's unlocked, he bends down and scoops me up before I can walk through, making me squeal. "Maxum! I'm too heavy now. Stop! You'll hurt yourself!"

He laughs as he makes it through the front door, kicking it shut behind him. "You'll never be too heavy for me, beautiful," he claims. One of the things I like about my apartment is the fact that I have a self-locking door. It's the only reason my dad let me move out, if I'm being completely truthful, though. The irony is that I'm in the townhouses that the Rebel Guardians own and manage, although I'm on one of the ends so I don't have stairs. Good thing, too, because my balance is kind of off these days and I could just see me flying ass over elbow down the stairs. Yeah, no thanks. He carries me into the bedroom then through to the master bath. "I figure we'll get cleaned up, then get dirty," he explains as he sets me down on my feet. "Then get cleaned up again. Rinse and repeat until you pass out, baby." I grin because the build-up of hormones has me nearly at combustion stage already and we're fully clothed! He starts the bath and gets the temperature just right, then tosses in some bath salts. I love that he's not afraid to get in with me despite my penchant for girly scents. Granted, before he leaves my place, he always showers so the guys won't give him shit, but when it's just us, he simply doesn't care.

"I think we've got too many clothes on for naked house day," I tease.

"Gonna fix that right now," he growls out, giving me a heated look.

"I think my underwear just melted," I confess, giggling.

"One less thing in my way then, huh?" he responds, slipping my shirt over my head before he unclasps my bra and slides the straps down my arms. "Fuck, Lil, your tits are so fucking luscious right now," he says, leaning in and licking the tip of first one nipple then the other. I feel my body responding and let out a soft huff. Maybe bigger boobs isn't such a bad thing based on how he's staring. "What was that for?" he asks, undoing my pants and sliding them and my panties down my legs.

"Just that little touch has me wet," I confess. I can feel my face heat and know I'm blushing. I mean, why should I be blushing? He's seen me naked before.

"Well, carrying you in and feeling your ass in my hands has me harder than a rock," he replies, placing a soft kiss on the inside of my knee. Damn, I had no idea that spot was an erogenous zone but suddenly, I don't give two flips about a bath, I want him buried so deep inside me that I feel him for days.

"Then what are you waiting for?" I question, waving at him while he stands there fully clothed. "Think we both have to be naked, or mostly anyhow, for anything to happen."

He grins at me before doing that thing that men can do where they're nude within seconds. If I could bottle that shit, I'd be a millionaire! "C'mon, baby," he says, leading me over to the tub which is just right. I step in and he gets in behind me, settling me against his chest. I can feel him pressed against my back and a shiver runs through me. "You cold?" he asks, picking up the bath sponge from the shelf.

"Not exactly. Kind of feel like I'm burning up."

"Let's see if we can get you a little hotter then, shall we?" he jokes.

By the time he's done washing me and himself, I'm a panting mess. Each touch, each caress, each kiss dropped on my skin has me moaning with need and desire. "Maxum," I whisper. "Can we go to bed now?" Without a word, he stands and gets out before helping me out. Then, instead of carrying me into the bed dripping wet in more ways than one, he proceeds to dry me... very thoroughly, I might add.

His hands now gripping my hips, he leans in and presses kisses across my burgeoning stomach. “God, I love you, Lily, and seeing you growing our baby has me all kinds of turned on.” Before I can respond, his head dips lower and he swipes his tongue across my folds. “Spread your legs a bit, Lil,” he commands, his voice raspy with need.

When I obey automatically, I moan because he proceeds to nuzzle against my pussy and suck lightly at my clit. “Fuck, Maxum, feels so good,” I cry out.

“You’re soaked, baby. Don’t think it’s going to take long for you, huh?” he teases, glancing up at me.

“Shut it, handsome, and make me come. I need to come on your tongue and then I want you to make love to me until I scream your name.”

“Gladly,” he replies. Suddenly, I’m lifted so my ass is now on the bathroom counter and he’s kneeling in front of me. I feel so wanton as I lean against the mirror, my legs now drawn up and my feet on his shoulders. His assault on my pussy is intensifying and I feel myself climbing higher and higher. When he adds two fingers to the mix and begins pumping them into me, I lose it, keening out his name as my pussy pulses around his digits. He doesn’t stop; no, he continues his ministrations until I'm coming again.

He finally gentles his touch and withdraws his fingers, then proceeds to lick them clean. "I think you're even sweeter than before," he murmurs before scooping me up and carrying me to bed.

Maxum

I PLACE US SO WE'RE SIDE-BY-SIDE SO I CAN KISS HER senseless. While I want nothing more than to plunge into her warm, wet depths, I know that right now, my control is at a bare minimum. Since I want this to last more than a few thrusts, I decide to slow it down a bit. Caressing her face, I say, "You have no idea what you do to me, Lily."

"Then show me," she replies, leaning in to kiss me.

Slow, wet kisses soon turn to hot, deep ones and I find myself rolling her to her back so I can see all of her and get to everything. She gives me a strange look when I grab a pillow and situate it under her hips so I say, "I read that this will help you since you're pregnant. We may need to experiment a bit more, if you're up to the task."

She grins up at me and replies, "Challenge accepted, biker boy." I chuckle before leaning in and capturing one of her nipples between my lips. I know they've become more sensitive and her moans let me know that she's enjoying the attention. I switch back and forth between the two, using my hand on the one that's not being sucked and licked.

As I move down her body, I marvel at the changes. I know she thinks she's gotten fat, but to me, she's the most precious thing in the world. I kiss and lick down her side where the faint stretch marks show until I reach our baby. "You need to take a nap now, little one, it's time for your daddy to love on your momma." Her giggles make me grin as I grab my dick and place it at her entrance. Sliding into her warmth, I have only one thought.

Home.

I'm home.

"Feels like it's been forever," I grunt out as I begin a slow, steady pace. Lily wraps her legs around my waist and the addition of the pillow has me going in even deeper.

"It has been forever, baby," she replies. "Please, move faster."

I increase my pace and on the downward thrusts, swivel my hips so I hit her G-spot. When I start feeling her pussy flutter, I realize that she was as ready for this as I was and I begin pistoning my hips even faster. As her back arches and her pussy clamps down on my dick, I let go, shouting her name as I pour months' worth of cum into her willing sheath.

I can still feel her pussy milking my dick when she reaches up and pulls my head down before she kisses me. Gentling my thrusts, I kiss her until we're both breathless, then pull back slightly and drop to my side, cradling her against me. "Love you, Lily," I murmur, brushing back some wayward hairs that have fallen in her face.

"I love you too, Maxum. Give me a few minutes and we can do that again. I'm curious about these other positions."

WE SPEND THE REST OF 'NAKED HOUSE DAY' BEING, WELL, naked. I've lost count of her orgasms and quite frankly, think my dick just might be broken. It's as if all the months of abstaining were built up until we hit today. Best fucking day of my life.

15

LILY

It has taken a month to get things organized, ordered and ready for our gender reveal party. During that time, Maxum used his body to help me pass the time. You'll never hear me complain over his techniques. Claree was so excited when I asked her to order the cut and cake. She gushed over being chosen with this secret, something she thoroughly enjoyed teasing DJ and Mom about every time she saw them.

Not once did she let it slip out, showing me that she was the right woman for the job. The Fallen Creek chapter of the Rebel Guardians made the trip down to celebrate with us. I know I would've been heartbroken had Luca and Gypsy not made the trip. The old ladies have tirelessly worked on the clubhouse, making it look like baby supplies and decorations have vomited over nearly every room. Even the kitchen wasn't safe! I have to give it to my dad though, he has taken it all in stride with a smile on his face. I'm positive that every time he went into his office, it was to curse one of them out without having to deal with their attitudes. He should be used to it by now, though. I mean, us kids did that many times when we were younger.

He's the best daddy a girl could've asked for.

"Let's get this party started," DJ bellows out to a bunch of moans and groans from the men. "Y'all are party poopers." She glares at each and every one of them. "I don't know about you all, but I wanna start shopping for the newest baby in the family. Grow up, pull up your big boy britches and deal." They all get somber expressions on their faces at her scolding. I so wanna be DJ when I grow up. She knows how to put all of these men in their places, but each and every one of them adore her and would do anything for her. They all say it's from fear, but I know better.

Maxum and I are seated in chairs in front of everyone and I am beyond anxious to open up the package that Claree is guarding in her hands. She's a warden with the secret and the box. Maxum has tried several times in the past couple of weeks to get her to break, but she refused. Watching him sulk was fun to watch; something tells me he's making up for his lost years when he couldn't be a child. Instead, he's portrayed one well by stomping his feet and arguing with her that it's his child and if he wants to know, if he can't wait a moment longer to make plans, then he should be informed. Their arguments have become entertainment to all of us, and each new emotion he's allowed himself to feel has made me think of a summer flower, whose opened up its petals, and is blooming.

"Is it time yet?" Maxum whines and once again all of the men crack up at his prepubescent behavior.

"Yes, Maxum, it's time," Claree sweetly answers using her tender, motherly voice with him. I hide my smile because it's the same one she uses with her kids.

"It's about damn time," he huffs. I reach over and pat his knee with my hand. He gives me a 'don't patronize me' look and I giggle.

Claree gently places the box in my lap and I start tearing into it. Maxum, not one to be outdone, rips at the tissue paper until a powder pink cut can be seen. “It’s a girl, Maxum!” I holler out.

“A girl, fuck my life. Axe, get the shotguns prepared!” His face has paled some, but I still see the excitement in his eyes.

“I didn’t use one on you,” Dad hollers out to him.

“That’s because I’m awesome,” Maxum replies. “But are you seriously telling me that a granddaughter with your daughter’s looks will be safe from all of the boys in town?”

“Cara, we’re leaving here and hitting the gun store,” Dad responds and the women all roll their eyes.

“There will be no shooting little boys, Braxton,” Mom scolds him.

“How about tasers, can we taser the little fuckers?” Smokey asks.

“Oh, my *God*!” I put my face in my hands to hide the laughter from them. There’s no need to encourage their behavior.

“Pepper spray works too,” Bandit announces.

"Somebody save my daughter!" I cry out through my hysterical laughter.

"You survived growing up with a bunch of overprotective, macho men, she will too," Mom encourages.

"She might, but no snot-nosed little fucker with a penis will," Maxum states.

"I'm taking our daughter and going into witness protection," I announce.

"Oh, love, you can't hide from me," Maxum says. "No matter where you go I will find you… both of you." He places his hand on my stomach and my eyes begin to water. "I'll never let either of you leave me."

Maxum

THIS TIME, I DON'T FREAK OUT WHEN THE TEARS FLOW from her eyes, sliding down her cheeks. This isn't pregnancy hormones or a hurt cry, this time it's for love.

"Maxum," she whispers before her lips crash down on mine.

"Get a room," Tig hollers out.

"No!" I hear all of my brothers shout in uniformed synchronization. Lily and I chuckle with our lips still glued to one another's. As we stare into each other's eyes, a feeling of euphoria wracks my body. She's what I've always needed, she's saved me from my past. I love this woman more than my own breath.

She is my everything!

It's been three months since our gender reveal party. We've since had a baby shower, decorated our daughter's room and have not had one day of peace from the old ladies. Every day there's been a shopping excursion; decorating the baby's room more than it already was, washing baby clothes, picking out her future day care… yes, that's really a thing, apparently. If they're not doing any of those listed items, then they're just sitting around, gossiping like a bunch of old hens. Now, I understand what my brothers have been bitching about for all of these years.

"Maxum, I think I'm in labor," Lily says, breaking me out of my reverie.

"Say what now? It's too soon!" I holler, standing up and rushing over to where she's standing in the mouth of the hallway. "How do you know?"

"I've been having contractions off and on for the last hour. It hurts, Maxum," she whines, face planting into my shoulder. I can hear her huffing and puffing. I hate seeing her in distress, labor is no joke.

"I'll call the doctor on the way to the hospital. Let's grab your bags and hit the road."

"I'm not ready," she cries.

"Me either." I wish I could join her in tears, but only one of us can break down at a time. The other needs to be strong and keep focused.

"BRAXTON HICKS," DR. SANDOVAL SAYS.

"Braxton whata?" I ask, perturbed at the outcome.

"It's Lily's body's way of preparing for childbirth. This could go on until the day she delivers, or sporadically come and go," she goes on to explain.

"This is just *practice*! Does that mean the pain will be worse later on?" Lily asks her and I see fear plastered all over her beautiful face.

"I'm not going to sugarcoat things for you, Lily. They will be more intense, and you'll feel them much more than you are now." Well, thank you, Dr. Sandoval! Now, I'm gonna have to deal with a somber Lil, who's always worried about the day labor comes on. She's gonna freak the fuck out!

"Great, that's just fabulous news," she pouts.

"I'm going to discharge you so you can go home and get some rest. The day is quickly approaching and you'll need all of your rest now. Once that baby comes, your days of sleeping in are over." Fucking hell. Seriously? I wonder if it's against protocol for me to duct tape the doctor's mouth shut.

After the belt thingies that allow us to hear our daughter's heartbeat are unwound from Lily's belly, they discharge her. I'm holding her hand in mine as we exit and a shadowy figure, hiding in the darkness, catches my attention. I turn my head in an attempt to see if I recognize whoever is standing there, only they've disappeared. Weird. Shaking my head, I pull Lily closer and hurry us to the car. Right now, she's my priority. I'll ignore the strange frisson of dread that shivers through my body.

16

MAXUM

It's been two weeks since Lily's false alarm with the Braxton-Hicks contractions. I'm lounging on the bed waiting for her to come out of the bathroom so we can watch one of the damn Hallmark movies she loves when I hear, "Maxum? I need you!" I jump up and rush to the bathroom door and fling it open, not bothering to knock since she hollered for me.

"What's wrong, baby?" I ask, looking around the bathroom. My eyes widen when I see the puddle of water beneath her feet at the sink. "Lily?"

"My water broke, Maxum. I think it's really time," she states calmly while stripping out of her wet nightgown. "Can you help me get cleaned up before we go?" I'm halfway out the door when her words stop me in my tracks. *Cleaned up*? We've got our daughter on the way, there's no fucking time!

"Lily, baby, we don't have time," I insist as I go back to grab her hand to drag her into the bedroom in order to dress her.

"Maxum! Yes, there is, dammit. I'm not even having any contractions that I can feel. Don't you remember the classes? First babies can take longer and I refuse to go anywhere like this! Shit, it's still leaking. I'm taking a shower first, then I'll be getting dressed. I'll wear a fucking pad or stuff a towel down there but I will be clean!" She's a pain in my damn ass sometimes. I don't know why she wants to get clean, only to get dirty again, while she labors.

Deciding not to argue with her, I start the shower, strip myself down, then get us both inside. I quickly wash us both then pull her out and have her dried off before she realizes what I've done. "C'mon, Lily, our little girl is coming," I say, rushing to her dresser and pulling out some clothes. When she doesn't move fast enough for me, I start dressing her, but stop when I hear a noise. Glancing up, I see she's laughing so hard that tears are pouring down her face. "Why are you laughing?"

"B-b-because you're acting a tad bit crazy right now! It's going to be okay, Maxum. Women have babies every single day. Now, get dressed, I think I can finish from here." Maybe women have babies every day, but this is a first for my woman and I want her where she can get help with the whole thing, not standing here bare ass naked.

I don't bother with my boxers. Instead I slip on jeans, socks, my boots and my cut and start toward the closet to grab the suitcase we've had packed for weeks now. "Aren't you forgetting something?" she sweetly asks.

"What?"

"Umm, maybe a shirt?" she teases, sitting down on the end of the bed so I can help put her shoes on. I glance down and see my bare chest and grin.

"Guess I'm a bit excited. Nervous as fuck, too, if I'm being honest," I reply. I don't want to see her in that kind of pain, but the stuff they use might possibly interact with her other medicines, so she decided, against my better wishes, mind you, to go as natural as possible.

"I'm ready, honey," she says. "Well, once you help me up, that is." My woman is all baby in the front and gets off balance. I hold out my hands and once hers are in mine, gently lift her to her feet before deciding, fuck it, and scooping her into my arms. "Maxum, I'm way too fucking heavy at this point," she chastises.

"You'll never be too heavy for this badass biker," I tease, leaning in and kissing her nose. "Now, c'mon, we've got a daughter to meet." I make quick work of getting us out to the truck then run back inside and grab the suitcase. It's baby time.

OKAY, MAYBE THIS LABOR SHIT IS LONGER THAN I thought it would be. We've been here for hours now. I keep running back and forth between the waiting room and Lily, to give the progress reports to our family. Dr. Sandoval was thankfully already at the hospital, delivering another baby when we arrived. She's been checking Lily frequently as she progresses. Despite the contractions increasing in strength, Lil is being a trouper. "Lily, are you sure you don't want any pain medicine?" I question after a particularly brutal contraction.

"No! It's not that bad," she lies as she slumps against the pillow.

I wipe her face, then move to her upper chest, wiping her down with a cool cloth. Then, I place a gentle kiss on her temple. "You're lying, Lily. Please tell me it's not worse than your headaches."

"It's comparable," she admits. Another contraction hits and she says, "I think we need the doctor, Maxum. I feel pressure down there, like I have to push."

Panic grips me when I see her clutching the sheets in her hands so hard that her knuckles turn white. "Nurse!" I bellow, running for the door. "Need some help in here. She wants to push." Several nurses, as well as Dr. Sandoval, rush into the room and I find myself relegated to the spot near her head.

Feeling clueless, I automatically do what I'm instructed and after what feels like an eternity has passed, but is in reality mere minutes, I hear the sweetest cry and Dr. Sandoval says, "Welcome to the world, baby girl!"

Lily

Torn between the agony happening between my legs and watching Maxum's face, I finally feel the pressure release as I push out our girl. I lose it when I see tears slipping down his face. My man has come so far, thanks not only to Dr. Graves and his brothers, but also his sheer determination not to repeat the cycle of abuse and neglect he endured. "Look at her, Lily," he says reverently, reaching out a finger and gently stroking her cheek. "She's beautiful."

I glance down but they placed her face down on my stomach so I can't really see anything except a naked, gunky baby. "How can you tell? She's ass up," I tiredly tease.

The nurse chuckles and Dr. Sandoval bursts into laughter. "That's one thing I never tire of hearing," she states. "New parents looking over their baby for the first time. How about we let the nurse take her and get her cleaned up and weighed, then we'll bring her back in to you, Mommy?"

I nod, suddenly exhausted. "Maxum, go with her and take lots of pictures," I plead.

"Have you decided on a name?" the nurse asks as she swaddles the baby.

"We have but are waiting to share it with our family," I reply.

"That group of bikers out in the waiting room?" she questions. I don't like the look on her face, but figure I'm just overly emotional from delivering a baby.

"My family? Yes, that's them." I put a little bit of a bite in my tone and she gives me a look I can't decipher.

"Then let's get this little one cleaned up so they can meet her. You coming, Daddy?" The nurse changes her tune from that of a judgmental tone to that of a sweet, caring individual. Fucking cunt, she has no room to judge my family based on their leather cuts alone. I hate when I have to put someone in their place. Judge a person by their appearance and you're missing out on who they are on the inside.

Oh, I don't like her, not one bit. She's batting her eyelashes at Maxum and practically ignoring me. Before I can say anything, Maxum leans down and kisses me before he whispers, "Thank you for this beautiful, earth-shattering gift, sweetheart. I love you."

"I love you too, handsome. Hurry back, please. I want to hold our girl."

After what feels like an eternity, Maxum, the nurse, and our baby come back. Thankfully, another nurse came in and got me cleaned up and moved to another room where I'll stay until we're discharged. Because if I know my family, they'll be taking tons of pictures and I don't want to look like a sea troll. "You ready for this?" he asks. When I nod, he sends a mass text so he doesn't have to leave, and we wait for the onslaught. Mom and Dad are first through the door, followed by Layne, Landon, Luca and Gypsy. Then the rest pile into the room until everyone is surrounding the bed.

"You going to tell us her name?" Dad asks, his voice gruff with emotion. Maxum and I grin at each other. We spent a lot of time tossing around names until we found one we both liked. It mimics mine in a way.

"Grandma, Grandpa, meet Violet Cassarah Bass," I say, lifting her slightly. I watch my dad's eyes grow wet as he reaches out and runs a finger down her cheek. Mom, however, bursts into tears before reaching for Violet.

"Let me see you, precious," she croons, cradling the baby close. "Oh, Lily, she's got your nose!"

"Gun shop, now," Luca growls out looking over Mom's shoulder. "Maybe you should consider reinforcements of some kind at the clubhouse, Dad. No sense taking chances. Can we put a chip in her? Lucy has one so if she ever gets lost, we can find her."

I roll my eyes at my brother's absurdity. "Luca, I am not chipping my daughter like a dog, for fuck's sake."

"Why not? It works, Lil. You should see the animals that are returned on our local discussion page because they're chipped."

"Who the fuck are you and what have you done with my badass brother?" I tease. "Because trust me, you are not acting like yourself in any way, shape or form."

"He's always been protective, Lil," Rae states. "But even I have to agree, this is a bit too much."

I glance around the room and see the women agreeing with me, while the men appear to be seriously pondering his suggestion. "No, just no. She's not getting microchipped. Nothing will happen to her, especially not with all of y'all keeping watch. Her daddy won't allow anyone to get that close."

"No, I won't," he advises.

"Nothing in this world is certain. You can't keep your eyes on her twenty-four hours, seven days a week, brother," Bandit adds. "I'll purchase her a bracelet and put a tracking device in it. She can wear it on her ankle or wrist, whichever you prefer."

"This is getting out of hand," I sigh.

"Now, that's something I could agree to," Maxum turns his attention to Bandit and states.

"Maxum," I gasp. "Please don't jump aboard the crazy train."

"Think about it, Lil. It would give us peace of mind and I wouldn't go gray worrying over her." Maxum is begging and pleading with his eyes for me to agree.

"No, absolutely not. I will not have my daughter being tracked and traced by you Neanderthals! She'll never get to go away with her friends without one of you tracking her every move. I won't allow y'all to strip her independence from her and have her growing up fearful that if she takes off the bracelet, something bad could happen to her. She'll be paranoid every day of her life. It's not happening, Maxum."

"She's a newborn, she doesn't have friends yet," Luca says.

"Not helping, Luca," I growl out, glaring at him. He grins at me as he crosses his arms over his chest. Fucking bikers!

"How about we enjoy this sweet girl and not worry about shit that'll never happen," DJ interjects. I grin at her; she's now my favorite.

17

MAXUM

I stare down in awe at Violet. She's having a hard time latching on, or some shit that I don't understand, plus she's developed jaundice, so she has to stay in the hospital a few extra days. Lily cried and pleaded to stay as well, but my insurance denied it since there was nothing wrong with her. Fucking bureaucrats. We're here for every visiting hour, and I probably have more pictures of my woman holding her than anything, but who the fuck cares?

I put a call in to Dr. Graves to give her the news and when she asked me how I was feeling, I was honest. I'm scared shitless that somehow, I'll become like my father, but both she and Lily have reassured me that already I'm different. The emotion that welled up inside when I first saw her and held her was almost overwhelming. Unconditional love, that's what Dr. Graves says it is, and it's something that my sperm donor apparently lacked.

"She looks better, doesn't she?" Lily whispers, taking Violet's hand in hers.

"She doesn't look as yellow, that's for sure." It freaked us both out when they brought Violet to us later that first day and she had turned a shade of yellow. The pediatrician explained that it happens and that they would put her in an incubator with a special lamp. Lily giggled the first time we saw her with her tiny blinders on to protect her eyes.

"When do you think we can bring her home?" she asks the nurse. I don't like this one because she seems a little too attentive, but try to shrug it off since I'm sure I'm in super-protective Daddy mode.

"Probably in the next day or so if her numbers continue to improve," the nurse replies.

"Good, I'll be glad to have both my girls under the same roof," I mutter. It still freaks me out that she's here by herself. Dr. Sandoval, upon hearing our concerns, showed us the bracelets that all new parents and their babies wear. It has a code on it so that's given me a measure of peace. It's still minimal at best because I'm not the one with my eyes on my precious girl.

"Do you want to feed her?" Lily asks. "Remember, we're doing skin to skin."

I grin because every time I feed Violet; Lily gets pissed off at whichever nurse is working. They're downright shameless, flirting with me with her right there. The only one who doesn't is the nurse neither of us care for which is strange to me. "You sure you can handle seeing all of this?" I ask, waving my hand down my chest.

She rolls her eyes and giggles. "I think I can deal," she replies. I know she's sad that she isn't able to breastfeed, but this means I get to share in all the nitty-gritty shit when it comes to taking care of our daughter. I will never tire of watching her little face and I swear, she smiles every time she's in my arms. Lily tells me it's gas, but I don't believe it. I think Violet recognizes my voice from all our tummy conversations.

Once I've settled into the rocker and start feeding my girl, I notice Lily snapping pictures. "We need to print some of these out," she says. "Maybe Bandit can help us do a slideshow or something."

"For what?"

"For when she gets married. You know, kind of like a memory book, only in video format," she states.

"Don't you think it's a little too soon to be marrying off our daughter?" The thought of it makes me sick. I don't want a grubby-handed chump touching my beautiful girl.

"Alright, Mr. Caveman. Just saying, our daughter will be allowed to date, make her own mistakes, and have a life."

"Says who? I make enough to support all of us as long as she wants to live under my roof," I reply, not taking my eyes off Violet.

"You going to offer the same to any sons we have?" she snarks. "Or just any daughters?"

I contemplate her question. I know we'll raise Violet and any other kids we have to be independent, but women should be protected as far as I'm concerned. "Let me get back to you on that, okay?"

Lily

THIS MAN OF MINE IS GOING TO DRIVE ME CRAZY! As much as I love my daughter, and I'm positive I'll love any other kids I have, I have no intention of living in a house full of women! Deciding to tease him a little, I say, "Guess you don't want any more naked house days then, huh? I mean, if the house is going to be overrun with kids, we can't exactly be prancing around nude."

"That's what grandparents are for, Lil. We send them all on a weekend getaway while we play," he smiles. Oh boy, he's got an answer for everything, and won't my parents be happy to get many weekends with their grandkids as we prance around our home naked. That'll go over great when I explain that one to them.

"Would love to see my dad's face when you tell him the reason the kids are coming over is so you can frolic naked with his daughter." The look of sheer horror that crosses his face has me laughing so hard that I feel tears slipping down my face.

"Why do we have to tell them the reason we want them to watch the kids?" he questions, clutching Violet a bit closer.

"You know how he is; do you *really* think he won't ask?" I shoot back.

"Fuck. Okay, maybe we'll hold off on a houseful for a little longer. We can still have naked house days then, right?" The hopeful expression he now has gets my motor running. This waiting thing is for the birds, but Rae told me it was important, so I'll do it.

"Maybe, but that's weeks away, handsome, so don't get any ideas," I warn.

I'M LYING IN BED WITH TEARS STREAMING DOWN MY FACE. Maxum is sound asleep next to me and I try not to wake him with my body's wracking sobs. I feel like a failure leaving my baby behind for the nurses to care for. It should be me, dammit! I'm her mother, I should be up all hours of the night feeding her, rocking her, singing her lullabies and holding her hand as she recovers from the yellow-tinged skin.

"Lil? Baby, what's wrong?" I hear him ask as his strong arms band around me, holding me tightly to his chest. I feel small butterfly kisses on my neck as he starts whispering words of love and encouragement in my ear.

"I miss my baby," I sob out as I continue crying into my pillow. He rearranges me so we're chest to chest and cradles my face in his hands, wiping away my tears.

“I do too, beautiful. We’ll be there as soon as those doors open and they allow us to visit with her. We’ll stay until they kick us out, Lil. I promise, she’ll be coming home with us soon.”

“I-I know, but I’m her momma, I need to be the one taking care of her.” I hiccup through my tears.

“And you will be. Once she’s all better, she’ll be nestled in your arms for the rest of her life,” he soothes.

I don’t know how many days I can do this — come home from the hospital without my bundle of joy in my arms. “Just hold me, Maxum, never let me go.”

“Never, Lil. I’ll never let you go.” He kisses my forehead and just holds me until I fall into an exhausted, emotionally drained sleep.

18

LILY

The next morning, I'm rudely woken up to a pounding on the front door. The only thing that has me moving is the frantic way the banging continues. "Somebody better be dead, or fixing to be dead, to be beating the door down that way," Maxum huffs in irritation as he slips into a pair of his jeans as I throw a robe over my pajamas.

“Who do you think it is?” I ask him as I scurry behind him to the front door.

“No idea, not many people bang on the door that way unless it’s an emergency,” he replies as he disengages the locks and pulls the door open. Standing on our front porch is an officer in uniform partnered with a man in a suit. “May I help you?” Maxum asks them as he tightly grips the door in his hand.

“Maxum and Lily Bass?” the man in the suit asks.

“It’s Callahan, Lily Callahan,” I answer, sticking my head through the space between Maxum and the open door.

“Are you the parents of Violet Bass?” he asks. What the fuck is going on?

“Yes,” Maxum grits out.

“May we come in?” suit man asks. This is driving me crazy, why is he being so aloof? Can’t he just spit out what he’s wanting to know and tell me why my daughter’s name just left his mouth?

“Let the men in, Maxum,” I calmly say to my old man. He looks ready to wrap his hands around these men’s necks and that won’t get us the answers we need.

“Fine,” he says between his gritted teeth. As the men enter

the room, my manners kick into high gear and I offer them a cup of coffee, or a bottle of water, which they both decline.

"Sir, ma'am, there was an incident at the hospital last night," he starts and I gasp as images of my baby pop into my head.

"What kind of incident?" Maxum asks. I can see the same worry I'm feeling sketched on his face.

"During shift change last night, someone cut off Violet's security bracelet and took her out of the hospital. We've been looking over the hospital's security surveillance and we saw a nurse bundling Violet up and walking out with her."

"Excuse me?" Maxum angrily shouts as he hastily stands up, clenching his fists.

"Do you know why a nurse would take your baby? Is there some sort of club rivalry going on?"

"This has nothing to do with my club!" Maxum yells, slamming his fist to his chest. "We are a group of law-abiding citizens; we don't deal in illegal activities. We work hard, and your chief of police is an officer in the club! You need to look outside of the club and any vendettas you've made up in your pea-sized brain!" Oh shit, Maxum is pissed and I fear that he'll end up doing something stupid and landing himself behind bars. I need to call my dad! Pronto.

"I-I'm gonna call my dad," I inform Maxum. He nods his head, but his glare is still firmly placed on the two intruders in our home.

Braxton

I'm sitting in my office when the phone rings. It's bright and early, and I'm surprised anyone is awake at this hour. I had a restless night and had a hard time staying asleep. Work usually helps me settle the restless beast, but something has been bothering me all night; nothing seems to be calming me down. Seeing that it's Lily, my smile grows wide. "Hey, sweetheart, how's that sweet grandbaby of mine today? Your mom plans to go out shopping, so we'll be up there a little after visiting hours begin."

Silence.

It's profound, setting my teeth on edge. I look at my phone to make sure the connection wasn't dropped. "Lily?"

"D-daddy, she's gone." I hear gut-wrenching sobs across the line and can vaguely hear Maxum bellowing at someone. Fear unlike anything I've ever known grips me. Nothing I faced in the military, or anything I've dealt with since starting the Rebel Guardians compares to the terror her words have instilled.

"Who's gone, Lily?" I question, already standing and going to my safe. I'm a licensed concealed carrier, but because we have so many kids in and out of the clubhouse, I typically lock it in the safe when I get here so there are no accidents.

"T-t-the baby," she stammers out.

Ice flows through my veins as dread grips my heart. I cup the phone before yelling, "Hatch! Chief! Law!" I know they've come in since the cameras picked them up and I watched in real time on my computer as they walked through the front doors. They run into my office, along with Smokey and Bandit, who I didn't see come in. I'm surprised and shocked to see several of the old ladies come running in behind them. No clue why they'd be here this early, but right now, that's not my focus so I push it aside. I put the phone down, and hit the speaker button on my phone. "Lily Bug, you're on speaker and we're all here. What happened? Talk to me, sweetheart."

I hear her gulping a few times and know she's trying to calm herself down. "We were sleeping when there was a knock on the front door. We jumped up and ran to answer. There were two officers there. Daddy, they said a nurse took Violet and left the hospital. We have to find her! Maxum is fixing to kick these officers' asses and I can't deal with him going to jail. Please come help me, Daddy. I don't know what to do!" she hysterically hollers out.

"We're on our way, baby. Try to hold it together. We love you," I tell her.

"O-o-okay, Daddy. Love you too." I disconnect the call and start to issue orders when I see Cara standing there, white as a ghost.

"Braxton?" Her voice is high and reedy and she's shaking. "What's going on? Why was Lily crying? Is it the baby?"

I go to her and pull her into my arms before saying, "Someone took the baby from the hospital, Cara."

Despite my arms being around her, she falls to her knees, screaming, "Find my grandbaby, Braxton! Find her! God, please, *please*, bring her back to us!"

"We got it, Axe," Bandit says, already opening up his tablet. "You and Cara get to Lily and Maxum. When we know something, we'll be there. This fucker won't get away with this."

"I'm calling Jonas," Law states. "With the two of you

doing your computer shit, we should have answers pretty fucking quick."

"Calling the office to see what's going on. I'm off today, but I'm going in so I can stay informed," Chief says, walking out the door. He stops and lightly touches Cara's shoulder. "We'll get her back, Cara."

"My God, why would anyone want to take an innocent baby? This doesn't make any sense," Cara sobs into my chest.

"I want Silas and Atticus on this! I want someone to pay for fucking with my family," I inform the room at large. "No one fucks with mine and lives to see another day." My anger is at a level I've never experienced before. I don't know what to do with all this vengeance running through my body.

"We don't work like that brother," Law says, and I can see his flabbergasted look at my words.

"We do now," I issue, ushering out my wife so we can go comfort our daughter.

"Do you want me to call Luca?" Smokey calls out as I begin to leave the room.

"No, I've got it," I respond.

Luca

I'M SOUND ASLEEP, GYPSY IN MY ARMS WHEN THE BLARING ring of my phone wakes me. Answering the phone without looking at the caller ID I say, "Someone better be fucking dying."

"Violet was kidnapped from the hospital," Dad says. My body suddenly becomes alert and alive at his explosive words.

"What!" I scream, startling Gypsy who wakes up.

"What is it, Luca?" she asks me.

"Get up and get dressed, baby. Someone took Violet from the hospital," I rush out as I begin dressing myself with one hand as the other clutches my phone. "Do we know anything?"

"A nurse took her, disabled her identity band, slipped out during shift change," he tells me. "That's all we know for now."

"I'm on my way. Tell Lily I'll be there as quickly as I can." Hanging up the phone, I say a silent prayer for my niece's safe return and that God is watching over her while in the clutches of this mad woman's hands.

My anger takes hold, and I couldn't care less that Tig has an adjoining room to mine as I grab the chair and throw it across the room, hitting the wall. We got hotel rooms while in town to be close to Lily while she was having the baby.

Tig

I HEAR A LOUD CRASH FROM LUCA'S ROOM WHICH JARS ME from sleep. "What the fucking hell?" I ask, jumping out of bed and rushing to the door that separates my room from his. I begin aimlessly banging on it until the door flies open and Gypsy is standing there. She's pale and my fear spikes.

"What's wrong? Is Luca okay?" I rush out the questions.

"Luca's fine. Someone kidnapped Violet from the hospital. We're getting dressed to head over to Lily's apartment now."

"I'll meet y'all out front in five." I briskly turn around and begin rummaging through my travel bag for fresh clothes. Skipping a shower this morning, I run in the bathroom, take a piss and brush my teeth. When I make it out front, Luca and Gypsy are already sitting astride his motorcycle with the engine running. I swing my leg over mine and rev the engine when she kicks to life.

"We'll get her back, brother." I emphasize this statement by pounding my fist to my chest.

"Damn straight we will, and someone's gonna pay!" he returns.

Fuck yeah, they will.

19

MAXUM

The officers make themselves at home while Lily and I get dressed and start brewing a pot of coffee. I have to keep myself busy, otherwise I'll be out on the road combing the city, knocking on every door in this town until I find Violet. The apartment door swings open and I see Braxton, Cara, Luca, Gypsy and Tig come strolling in. Anger and fear are laced on each one of their faces. For the first time since I woke this morning, I take a much-needed breath… one I hadn't realized I'd been holding in until they walked through the door.

"Any word?" Axe turns his head toward the detectives as he asks this question.

"We're still combing through the hospital's footage. The only perpetrator we've seen is the nurse, one who used a fake name and records to get the job. They were professional documents and her references checked out. The administrators thought they were hiring an educated, professional nurse. Once we can ID her, we'll be able to track her down."

"Can we see the footage?" Tig asks.

"It's an active case, we aren't able to share that with you at this time," detective shit for brains answers.

"Call Chief," Axe orders Tig.

"On it," Tig replies as he pulls out his cell phone and walks back outside.

"Sir, you can't use your contacts. It's illegal to involve you and your men in my investigation."

"Watch me," Axe replies, and I step behind him to show I've got his back. Luca follows my lead.

“What’s everyone sitting around for twiddling their thumbs?” Hatch enters the apartment and asks.

“Because dick for brains is stalling in his investigation. He doesn't want us involved,” Axe answers.

“Tough titty,” Hatch responds. “Is there a reason you’re here? You’ve informed the family; your job is done. Hit the road.” He throws his thumb over his shoulder.

“We are in the middle of questioning the parents,” the brassy-balled fucker sneers.

Tig comes strutting through the door wearing a grin on his face. His phone is on speaker and I can hear Chief’s voice issuing orders from the other end of the line. “I’m in the apartment, Chief,” Tig informs him.

“Detective Shaw, why are you there harassing my family instead of out on the streets, locating this missing baby?” Chief sounds stressed, pissed and knowing his different tones of voices the way I do, I know this is one that implies this man needs to shake his ass and get moving.

“I’m questioning the parents, sir,” Detective Shaw grits out. It’s apparent he has no respect for Chief and doesn’t care for him too much. I can’t help but wonder if it’s because of his involvement with the MC.

“Are they suspects?” Chief asks him.

"Parents are always the first to be suspected. I have to rule them out." This guy is cruising for a bruising and I hope I can give him his first. He deserves a black eye for his outward rudeness directed towards us.

"Is there a baby there?" Chief is on a roll with putting this man in his place and I'm loving it.

"No, sir."

"Then get your ass away from them and go find my niece!" Chief bellows before disconnecting the line.

"I suggest," Axe grounds out, "that you find out who this nurse is and bring home my granddaughter without a scratch on her little body, understand?"

"Are you threatening me?" Detective Shaw puts his hand on the holster of his gun.

Finally, my resolve snaps and I lowly state, "It will be the last mistake you ever make." All eyes swing to me when the last word leaves my mouth.

"I could arrest you for that threat alone," Detective dipshit says to me.

"And he'll be out within the hour. Don't threaten my men," Axe demands.

"I think it's time you follow orders from your chief and

vacate the premises," Hatch advises him. "You've been given your orders, be a good puppy and do as commanded."

"Fucking hell," Lily whispers. "Can we just find my baby, *please*?"

"Oh, she'll be found and home by tonight. Won't she detective?" I disrespectfully spit out.

"I'll do my best." He stands and scurries out of the apartment with the uniformed officer trailing behind him with a smirk on his face. Seems his coworkers think as lowly of him as we do.

Lily

Mom and I stand there with our jaws hanging wide open. I've never seen the men in my life act like this before, and it's a side of them I hope I'm never on the receiving end of. "Well, that was… interesting," Mom says and I have to agree with her.

"Have you ever?" I ask, waving my hand in the general direction of where the men are standing.

"Never."

"Me either," I answer.

"I've never seen your dad so… scary," Mom tells me.

"Nope. Not even that time Rae and I snuck out to go to that party Dad and Hatch said we couldn't attend." Dad had never really punished me before that day, but I was in big trouble and he not only took all of my possessions away from me, leaving me in a room with a bed and dresser only, but his disappointment in me, that hurt more than anything he could've done or said. "I feel like I need to be doing something other than just sitting here."

"I know, baby, but there's not much we can do," Mom compassionately replies.

"Is there anything at all I can do to help, Lily?" Gypsy wraps her arm around my shoulder in support.

"I don't think so." I shrug my shoulders.

"Should I make everyone breakfast while the men come up with a plan?" Gypsy asks Mom more than me.

"I don't think I could eat a bite," I answer.

"That would be very helpful, dear. There's no telling when the men will get another chance to stop and eat once they start searching," Mom says to her. I feel bad, because all I was thinking about was myself.

"Sorry, she's right," I apologetically state.

"You have nothing to apologize for," Maxum growls out as he comes up beside me and pulls me into his arms. "We will be getting her back, Lily. I vow this on my life."

"I know," I brokenly whisper. I know I'm a hot mess, with my bedhead hair and tears that won't stop, but I simply don't give a fuck.

Maxum

My phone begins ringing in my pocket. Pulling it out, I see Chief's name flashing on the display. "You got something?"

"I'm watching the footage, there's something familiar about this nurse. I just can't put my finger on it. Can you grab the guys and head on down to the station?" he asks me.

"Be there shortly," I respond. "Chief wants us down at the station as soon as possible," I announce to my brothers.

"Did he say why?" Axe asks.

"Something about the nurse being familiar or something. I told him we'd be there quickly," I tell him.

"Then let's roll," he replies. Luca, Axe, and I kiss our old ladies and exit briskly. We don't have time to lose, she could be in another state by now.

"SON OF A MOTHERFUCKING *BITCH*!" AXE SCREAMS OUT AS we see a clear picture of the nurse's face.

"Do you know who that is Axe?" I ask, pointing to the screen.

"That's Daria, Lily's mom," he angrily spits out.

"That woman didn't fuck with my old lady enough in life, now she has to steal her baby!" I scream, pissed and worried about my daughter and how Lily's going to take the news.

Hatch picks up his phone and places a call. "Bandit, get with Jonas, find out everything you can about Lily's mom's activities and whereabouts," he issues the order. After Bandit says something, Hatch grunts and hangs up the phone.

"Where was the prospect guarding Violet at while all of this took place?" Tig asks. I had forgotten about him; the fucker better be dead. There's no excuse to leave his post other than death itself.

"Don't know, but I'm fixing to find out," Hatch says, excusing himself from the room.

20

MAXUM

We've all reconvened at the clubhouse, making plans for when we discover where Daria's been hiding out in town. What irks me the most is that she's been living here, under our noses, making plans to destroy our lives. I haven't shared this with Lily as of yet. I want to be there for her when she hears the news. I know she's going to break down, needing to know why. I want to have those answers for her before sharing.

The office phone begins ringing and Axe answers, immediately putting it on speaker phone. "Silas, you're on speaker."

"Good, you all need to hear this," he huskily responds. "I've had an issue I've been dealing with for a while now, seems we have a common enemy."

"That would be?" I insert myself into the conversation. Axe gives me a wayward look but doesn't reprimand me for my interference.

"Seems Lily's mom is actually working with someone else. One who is into skin trading, drugs, weapons, kidnapping and selling babies to the highest bidder." When the last item on his list leaves his mouth, fire burns in my gut. Is this why my baby was stolen? Fucking hell, I knew this woman didn't give the first fuck about Lily, but this is her granddaughter and she's going to sell her? What the actual fuck!

"Who's this person she's working with?" Axe questions Silas.

"We haven't discovered who it is, yet. We were interrogating Rae's ex and his dad, but they feared this person more than death. Whoever it is, they're good, really good.

Jonas and Raven have been searching high and low and still haven't discovered who it is. They've worked on this night and day, but we have been able to link Daria to this person."

"Why is it, that this the first time I'm hearing about a new player in town?" Axe bewilderedly asks.

"We thought we had it under control," Silas says in an irritated tone.

"Being upset at each other is getting us nowhere," Hatch interjects. "Let's find Violet and hash everything else out later." He's in enforcer mode, which is rare, but when he is, you know heads are about to roll.

"Does this mean you have leads on where Daria is?" I interrogate Silas.

"Maxum?"

"Yeah, it's me," I answer.

"You're not going to like this. It's gonna hit home and hurt you deeply." He prepares me, but nothing could ever help me get ready for the next words that leave him. "Her boyfriend is one Killian James Bass."

Shock.

Anger.

Ghosts.

My past has come up to rear its ugly head. My father, he's dating Lily's *mom*? Is he in cahoots with her stealing my daughter from the hospital? I wouldn't put it past him, he's a monster hiding in human form.

I'm gonna kill him!

"Maxum, breath, man." Luca comes up and places a hand on my shoulder.

"Did he help her take my baby?" I ask with a calm facade.

"Maxum —" Silas says.

"Tell me," I quickly cut him off before he can say more.

"Yes," he hesitantly answers.

"I want his head on a spike. I want him to suffer, to die a slow, painful death," I announce. I begin pacing back and forth, feeling despair like I never have before.

"He will. I promise he will," Silas vows.

"We have to find him first," Axe continues. "Any leads we can follow?"

"I have a few. Let me follow the leads and find the right one and I'll call you back," Silas informs.

"We'll be waiting," Axe says before disconnecting the line.

"I need a drink," I say as I flop down in my chair.

"I'll get you a shot," Tig states as he walks over to the small bar area that resides in this room. Now I know why it's here, I always wondered if anyone ever drank from it.

"Just the one, you need a clear head when we go hunting," Axe orders me. "And there's no place in this town that's safe for them, not with all of us looking. I'll burn this motherfucking town to the ground to find our girl."

"One's all I need to calm my frayed nerves," I mutter. Right now, Axe is someone I don't recognize, and the older brothers are as well. Most are former military, so I know they've seen some shit, but our club has always been on the up-and-up.

Lily

"What do you think is taking them so long to come back?" I ask no one in general.

"If they have a lead, they'll follow it before coming here," Mom replies.

"Wouldn't they tell us first if they've found something out?" My mind is racing with question after question.

"I doubt it," Gypsy states. "If it was me, I wouldn't. I'd follow all leads before giving Luca false hope."

"This is so jacked up!" I scream. "Who is crazy enough to steal another woman's baby? I just don't get it."

"That's because you're a caring, loving human being, Lily." Mom sits down next to me. She pulls me into the embrace of her loving arms. This usually comforts me, but it's not working today.

"I just want her back safe and sound, Mom."

"I know you do, baby. We all do," she chokes out. I look up and see that both my mom and Gypsy are silently crying.

"This is a nightmare I can't seem to wake up from. I need it over, I want whoever stole my baby to pay. But most of all, I need to place my eyes on her. Make sure she's safe, unharmed, not full of fear because Maxum and I aren't with her." I begin bawling uncontrollably.

Mom simply holds me, rocking me in place. I cry myself to sleep, but Mom never once lets me go.

I slowly come awake to voices in the background. They're hazy, then it dawns on me that Mom is on the phone with someone. "Who is it?" I ask, rubbing the sleep from my eyes.

"It's your dad. They're waiting on a few leads to pan out. Maxum has been trying to get a hold of you, he's been continuously calling your phone and is frantic because you weren't answering. Dad called me to check on you for him."

"I didn't hear it ring," I hazily say.

"I just went and checked, it's silenced," Gypsy says, handing my phone over to me.

"Thanks," I gratefully say. "Tell Dad to let Maxum know I'll call him back after I use the bathroom." I stand up and walk away, my bladder screaming in protest.

Once I use the bathroom, I take a few minutes to get myself cleaned up then get dressed. Closing the bedroom door, I call Maxum. "Do you know anything?" I ask. I feel my leg jumping because of the nervous energy flowing through me, but I can't stop.

"Tracking some leads, baby. Got the Nelsons working on it as well." I nod even though he can't see me. I don't know the Nelson brothers, but I do know, from things I've overheard, that they deal with the dregs of society and 'take out the trash' which is what Tig was saying one day when I was walking by. As soon as they saw me, they changed the subject, but that's okay.

"Maxum? Is it awful of me that I want them to pay? I want them to hurt? Hell, I don't know that I want the authorities to deal with it all, either," I confess. Since getting the news, all I can think about is flaying the person's skin from their body piece by piece. Gory? Probably, but right now, they've got my sweet baby girl and I have a sinking feeling it's for nefarious reasons.

"They'll pay, sweetheart," he vows. "And trust me, they better pray that the cops find them and not us or the Nelsons, because they won't bother anyone ever again."

"Good." If that makes me an evil bitch, so be it. "When y'all find them, I want my time with them too." I may be small, but I have skills that my family has taught me for self-defense purposes and I want to use them so I can make whoever took Violet hurt.

"Not sure that'd be a good idea," he cautions.

"Will y'all be there too? Yes, of course you will, so I'll be perfectly safe," I advise. "But I need this, Maxum. I need to look that person or those people in the eye, hurt them then spit on them and tell them they lost."

I hear him sigh and know he's running his hand through

his hair. “If that’s what you need, that’s what you’ll get. I’ll be sure to tell your dad, okay?”

I laugh but there’s no humor laced behind it. “I’m sure he’s ready to burn the town down.” I saw how angry he was earlier and as protective as he is with all of us, the kidnapper has no idea that they’ve unleashed a roaring beast.

“You have no idea,” he replies. “Baby, go get some rest but keep your phone on you. And please, eat something.” My man knows me too well; I haven’t been able to eat anything because I’m afraid I’ll throw it right back up and with the beginnings of a headache, I don’t want to risk it.

“I will. I’m sorry, Maxum,” I say.

“Why are you apologizing, Lil?” he asks. I can hear the confusion in his voice.

“Because we couldn’t bring her home. If we had been able to, this wouldn’t have happened.”

“Lily Callahan, soon-to-be Bass, you are not responsible for this!” he roars into the phone.

“Did… did you just propose?” I question.

“Well, kind of, but you’re missing the point, dammit! The blame is on the kidnapper’s shoulders, not yours and not mine. Do you understand?”

Oh, I love when his voice gets all masculine, dark, and growly, then I let out a sob because here I am, getting turned on by his voice and our daughter is in the hands of a madman!

"Baby, why are you crying?"

"B-b-because that's the voice you use when we're making love and it turns me on. I feel guilty right now because I shouldn't be thinking like that with Violet missing," I cry. I must be hearing things! The blasted man just *chuckled* for fuck's sake! "Maxum? Are you laughing at me?"

"Not really, Lil. It's just that you do that to me whenever you're around so it's good to know I've got that same effect is all."

I roll my eyes even though he can't see me. "You've always had that effect on me, Maxum, and you damn well know it! Now, quit stalling and go find my baby!" I insist.

"Love you, Lily," he says.

"Love you more, Maxum."

Maxum

I HANG UP THE PHONE AND SIGH. I DIDN'T TELL HER WHO has Violet because I need to have her in my arms before I shatter her world. I don't understand what her birth mother wants with our baby; she sure as fuck hasn't been around Lily since she was a tiny baby. I know Axe did all he could and Nan was undoubtedly a huge help, but my woman didn't have a real mom until Cara came into the picture. I smile when I think about how that particular woman became the glue for that family. Not only that, but with her standing beside Axe, I've seen him calm significantly over the years. Well, except for right now, but fuck, that's his little girl's baby and I feel confident that if he feels he has to burn the town down, he'll do so without any hesitation.

Walking back in to where everyone else is sitting, I say, "She's holding on, but barely. Do we have any kind of a plan yet?"

Law looks at me and replies, "The Nelsons are on their way here so we can hash out a plan of action."

I bite back a groan because the three brothers are forces of nature, and if I'm being truthful, mostly assholes. But right now, I'll take all the help we can get if it allows me to bring my baby girl home to her momma. Speaking of which, I see Axe off to the side and motion for him to follow me outside. Seeing as I kind of told Lily she was going to be my wife, I need to get his permission. "What's up, Maxum?" he asks as we step outside.

"I want to get your permission to ask Lily to marry me," I reply.

"I was wondering when you were going to talk to me about making her an honest woman," he states, folding his hands across his chest.

"Planned to do it before now, honestly, but with the appointments with Dr. Graves and the homework she had us doing, it went to the back burner. I didn't mean to offend by not asking sooner, Axe." At this point, I'll fucking grovel if I have to because she'll be my wife one way or another.

The grin that crosses his face throws me off, especially when he says, "I've got Nan's original engagement ring from my dad; would you like to have that to give her? It probably needs to be sized down since Lily's hand is smaller than Nan's."

"If you think she'd like that, then yes, I would. Thanks, Axe." He pulls me in for a man hug, slapping my back a few times. "Speaking of Nan, how is it that she's not here?"

"I called Gino and told him what was going on and asked him to keep her busy cooking stuff. She'll be here soon, I imagine, so be prepared."

I nod because Nan is like a tornado and you can always feel the whirlwind whenever she's around. Since she was so instrumental in raising Lily, this is probably killing her too. "How is… how did she take it?"

"She was all set to take Gino's gun and go out looking herself, but he managed to talk her down and tell her that the best way she could help was to make sure that we had food." His words force a chuckle out of me because I can visualize her saying that very thing.

Axe looks around and asks, "You two planning to stay at the townhouse long?"

"No, been working with Jaxson on a place. It's not too far from the clubhouse, but is out in the country. It needed some renovations and updating, so he and his crew have been working non-stop to get that done for me."

"Does Lily like it?" he questions. At my look, he says, "She has no clue."

"Well, no, she doesn't, but it's one she always comments on whenever we're on the way to the clubhouse. It finally came up for sale and I snapped it up without telling her. We won't have a mortgage because the owner was motivated to unload it fast."

"I know the one you mean. It's a big farmhouse, Maxum. How many kids are you two planning to have?" I think of naked house day, having to find a babysitter so I can continue to enjoy those days with my woman, and can feel my face redden as my president stares me down.

"Uh, we haven't really decided," I reply. He quirks his eyebrow at me and I continue, "We want to enjoy Violet for a little while before we add to the family. Plus, I want her to be my wife before we have any more kids." I can see that my answer appeases him because he nods, slaps me on the back again and heads back into the house without another word.

21

MAXUM

Waiting for the Nelsons to arrive is going to give me gray hair. Axe went inside to check on the guys and I'm sitting here outside, watching the road that leads to the clubhouse, like I can make them make it here quicker. I'm not always the most patient person to begin with and knowing that they have information that will lead us to my daughter has me feeling antsy. I jump and nearly yell out when a hand clasps my shoulder. Turning, I see Jaxson standing there. "You doing alright, brother?" he questions.

"What do you think, Jax? My baby is out there in the hands of that motherfucking sadistic prick and Lily's fucking birth incubator. To say I'm worried as hell is an understatement, especially after hearing the shit that those two are likely involved in. If Violet's hurt, there's nowhere on earth that'll be safe for them, I promise you that much."

"We got your back, brother. Thought I'd see if I could take your mind off things and show you the latest pictures of the house," he replies, pulling out his phone. At my nod, he opens up his camera roll and hands it to me. Jax has the ability to make anything come to life. Whether it's a car, bike or building things, everything he touches comes out like a spun thread of gold. I love that he not only works with me at the garage but also has his hands in deep with construction. He's a man of many talents, and I'm honored he's taken up the role of heading the crew working to make our house the perfect home for my growing family.

As I scroll, I'm amazed at the attention to detail in each picture. He's taken every one of my suggestions and combined them with what he knows Lily likes. "She's going to love it," I finally say, handing him his phone.

"How about you?" he asks.

"She's my home, man, so wherever she is, I'm good," I admit. "But I fucking love what you did in the master bedroom. Is that a custom-sized bed?"

"Yeah, thought you guys would appreciate the extra room, especially once Violet gets older and wants to come crawl in with y'all because she's scared," he says. I grin because knowing my woman, if our girl gets scared, she'll have her in with us in a heartbeat.

"Good idea. When do you think it'll be ready?" I ask.

"Well, I left a crew there to keep working but I'm obviously going to be here for y'all. I'd say if all goes well, maybe the next week or so."

"Appreciate it, Jax, more than you know."

He's about to say something else when we see the Nelsons pulling in. It's about fucking time! Of course, I'd never say that to them because they'd likely shoot first and ask questions later. "Everyone here?" Silas asks as they walk toward us.

"Yeah, inside," I reply, grabbing the door. Normally a prospect would be here, but when we located the little asshole who was supposed to be keeping a watch on my daughter, we found out he had slipped out for a smoke and a fuck with one of the nurses. Fearing for his life when

Axe heard, Hatch sent him home with instructions to think about whether or not the Rebel Guardians was what he honestly wanted, because it we are about loyalty, family, and brotherhood, and he didn't portray any of those qualities by worrying more about getting his dick wet than my little angel. I don't think we'll see him again, but if we do, I'm punching him for his sheer stupidity. I'm pretty sure that Luca will take a shot or two as well. Hell, I wouldn't be surprised if the rest of them lined up and beat the shit out of him at this point!

I follow them inside and when Axe sees, he pulls several tables together. "Y'all, have a seat," he commands, his president voice on full display. "What do y'all have?" he questions Silas. Silas' brow raises at Axe's tone, but my president doesn't back down. We may not deal in the things that other clubs do, but no one should ever mistake us for a group of pansy-assed pussies.

"Seems that they've been around for the past six months or so from what Jonas and Raven have been able to find. You know, of course, that Daria lied about her credentials and got a job at the hospital in the maternity ward. Not sure that Maxum's old man is aware of what her contacts are involved with because the research on him shows he's basically a bum." Silas shoots me an apologetic look and I shrug.

"He wasn't much more than that when I was a kid," I advise. "Glad to see some things never change." That last part might be a bit sarcastic, but all that asshole ever did was impregnate my mother, then run her off. Other than that, he was a miserable prick intent on breaking the two of us down until he eventually succeeded with her.

"Jonas checked other cameras nearby and Killian was driving at the time the baby was taken. He followed them to a house just on the outskirts of town, and we've got some of our guys out there watching to make sure they don't leave and no one else approaches." When I see Silas take a deep breath and look at Atticus, I brace myself, because whatever's coming next isn't going to be good.

Atticus glances at all of us and gives a slight almost imperceptible nod toward Axe and then me. I realize when Jaxson and Talon come up behind me and place their hands on my shoulder, then see that Hatch and Chief are doing the same to Axe, that they expect whatever bombshell they're going to drop will have us losing our shit. "I'm good," I mumble so only the two can hear me.

"Okay, so while Jonas was tracking them through the town's cameras, Raven was out on the dark web," Atticus says. When everyone but Bandit looks clueless, he pulls his hand through his hair and states, "The dark web is where the ugly shit is, y'know, the child molesters and what-not. The people who sell women and children." A cold dread seeps into my bones at his words.

"They're planning to *sell* my daughter?" I hiss out between clenched teeth.

Silas nods. "They've already got pictures up and bidding has started," he admits.

I'm not sure who is louder, Axe or me, but it takes every single brother to hold us back and keep us from destroying the common room in the clubhouse. "I can't tell Lily this shit," I whisper, finally slumping down in my chair. "This'll kill her." Not like I'm much better right now; my heart is pounding so hard in my chest that I'm having a hard time hearing what everyone is saying around me.

"We've got a plan," Silas says, breaking into my internal reverie.

"Let's hear it," Axe growls out. Both Hatch and Chief are still behind him and I can see the struggle he's undergoing to regain a semblance of calm, because I'm doing the same.

"Like I said, we have a few guys who are right there watching to make sure they don't leave with her again, and no one comes in. We want to get out there, secure the two of them, and let y'all get the baby back where she belongs," Silas states.

"Wait, so we're not going to be handling things?" Axe barks out.

"No. We need to find out who the fuck they're working for, or at least, who she's working for so we can shut that shit down. Y'all have bigger priorities, namely, getting your granddaughter back to the hospital to be checked, and reuniting her with her parents," Atticus replies.

I don't like it, not one bit. I want to put a hurting on them, well, at least my old man. But I also want Violet back under the hospital's care since she still has jaundice, and I want to be able to look my woman in the eyes and tell her that our girl is back. If that means I can't have the justice I long for, I have to presume that the Nelsons will ensure that there's plenty of pain involved in their interrogation of my sperm donor and the cunt who birthed Lily. When Axe starts to say something, I put my hand up. "Axe, I get it, trust me, I do. I'd like nothing more than to beat the fuck out of my old man for all he put me and my mom through, and while it goes against everything I believe in, I want Daria to hurt as well for causing my woman this unfathomable pain. But Violet's the priority and she wasn't left at the hospital just because the nurses didn't want to let her go. She needs that lamp thingy and the sooner we stop discussing this and head out, the sooner she can get the treatment she needs."

Axe takes a deep shuddering breath before he nods. "Fine. Let's get ready to roll. I think we need to take the cages so we can get there without them realizing."

"I'll send you the address," Silas states, standing.

"Silas?" Axe calls out.

"Yeah, man?"

"Tell Jonas and Raven we appreciate everything they've done to help with this. It won't be forgotten."

Silas doesn't reply, he merely waves his hand in acknowledgement as he and Atticus head to the door.

Lily

I'm pretty sure I'm going mad at this point. In order to keep from going out of my mind, I've been puttering around the house, cleaning and straightening, even though it's already spotless. "Lily, honey, come sit down and eat something," Nan says, coming up to me and wrapping me in her arms. "You need to keep your strength up so when Violet gets back, you're able to be with her." Nan showed up here earlier with bags of groceries in her and Gino's arms. She's been cooking up a storm ever since. The house smells divine with all of the aromas in the air, but it doesn't entice my hunger.

"Nan, I can't eat. The thought makes me want to puke," I admit. Plus, my headache has gotten steadily worse, something I've had a hard time hiding from my mom and my girls.

"Look at me, Lily," Nan commands. I turn and look at her, tears once again slipping down my cheeks. She runs her hand over my cheek and asks, "You've got a headache, don't you, child?"

"Yeah, Nan," I finally break down and admit.

"Let's get your medicine and feed you then." She says this as if it's finalized and I have no say so in the matter.

"Nan, I don't want to fall asleep! What if… what if they call?"

"Sweetheart, do you honestly think if they call we won't wake you up? No, we wouldn't do that to you. Now, listen to Nan and we'll get you all fixed up."

I trudge along behind her into the kitchen where my mom and Aunt DJ are sitting drinking coffee. "Let me get you a plate, Lily," Mom says, standing.

"I've got it, Cara. Can you go grab her medicine? She's got

a headache starting," Nan says. Mom shoots me a look that I try to avoid as I sit down at the table.

"Why didn't you say something, Lily?" Aunt DJ asks, confusion on her face.

"I didn't want to miss it if they called to say they found her," I begrudgingly admit.

"Honey, we won't let that happen. We'll wake you up, I promise," she asserts.

I nod because in my desire not to miss anything, it's gotten worse and I hope I can eat something so I don't throw up. They're all used to it by now, though, and Aunt DJ gets up and grabs an ice pack from the freezer before wrapping it in a towel and placing it on the back of my neck. "Thank you," I whisper. She leans in and kisses my forehead.

"Lily, we love you and we love that baby. Now, you eat something and then go lie down. I'll call Hatch and see if there's any news yet," she replies. I hide my smile because despite her sometimes gruff attitude, she's got a heart of gold and would do anything for any one of us.

It doesn't take long to eat a sandwich and take my medicines and before I know it, I'm lying in my bed. Rae comes in and closes the blackout drapes, then crawls in behind me and wraps her arms around my waist. "It's gonna be okay, Lil," she whispers. "We've got y'all."

"Couldn't do this if y'all weren't here," I reply, my voice already slurring as the medicine takes effect. "Don't let them leave me out of stuff, Rae. Promise me."

"I promise, Lily."

I WAKE UP REFRESHED AND EAGER TO HEAD TO THE hospital before reality intrudes once again. She's gone. My sweet baby girl is in the arms of someone who has evil intentions. While I don't know that for sure, it's the only reason someone would kidnap an infant as far as I'm aware. The club is a legit one, they have no enemies and in fact, have what a lot of clubs would consider allies located throughout the country. I smile a bit at that because that was my dad's vision — to create a brotherhood. I just hope the brothers have him and my old man tight in their grasp because as crazy as this is making me, I know those two are probably about to lose their ever-loving minds. I almost feel sorry for the person who did this… almost.

Getting up, I head into the bathroom to take care of business. Seeing my puffy eyes, I shrug, because until Violet is back in my arms, I suspect the tears will continue to flow. As I walk into the living room, I see everyone watching me. “Did you hear anything?” I ask, my voice coming out all raspy.

“They know where she’s been taken and they’re headed there now,” Mom says, coming over and pulling me into a hug. “It’s almost over, sweetheart,” she whispers. “You’ve been so strong through all of it.”

“Not really, Mom. I can’t keep from crying,” I admit as fresh tears trickle down my face.

“Eh, that’s the hormones bouncing through you,” Aunt DJ says, waving her hand. “You’re a strong woman, Lily. Many would be curled up in a corner, sobbing. You’ve been cleaning and all that shit, even with one of your headaches.”

“But I’m still crying,” I point out, wiping my face.

“It’s the dust,” Gypsy chimes in. “Does it to me all the time.”

I can’t help it, I giggle, then clasps my hand over my mouth in shock. “It’s okay to laugh, Lily,” Nan says. “We’re just waiting on them to call to say they’ve got her back then we’ll head to the hospital.”

“I need to go get ready,” I say, turning and heading back to the bedroom. I need a shower for sure and I know it’ll help me with the last little bit of the headache, like it always does.

“Make it quick, honey. Your uncle called about fifteen minutes ago and said they were nearly there.” I screech and start running, pulling my hair up in a messy bun so it doesn’t get wet.

22

MAXUM

The house they're hiding out in is a nondescript shack in the middle of nowhere. This works to our advantage since each house sits on a couple of acres of land and the closest neighbor won't be able to hear their screams of anguish. I take a deep gulp of air into my lungs as I try and control my wavering composure. I made promises before we headed here, and I intend to keep them, but I'm struggling to hold the anger at bay. Knowing my daughter is in there, waiting to come home to her family, has me wanting to rush in, blow both of their brains out and leave with my bundle of joy wrapped tightly in my arms. I'm not sure that I'll be able to take my eyes off of her for a long time to come once I have her back.

"Maxum, are you gonna be able to do this?" Talon questions.

"No choice, brother. It is what it is, my main priority is getting my girl out of this, unharmed. Nothing else matters," I lie through my gritted teeth.

"Oh, she's coming out without a mark on her," Axe ensures. "I'll accept nothing less." The look on his face and shining from his eyes lets me know he's in the same boat as I am. He wants to wrap his hands around Daria's neck and squeeze the life from her the same way I want to rip my father's head from his body.

"Y'all ready?" Silas comes over and joins our small huddle. "My guy just witnessed Daria put the baby down to bed. She's in the far left room. Maxum, you and Braxton head right to her and get her out. The rest of us will tie up the loose ends." What he means is, we get Violet out and they'll hogtie and put a small beatdown on my father and Lil's mom.

"Silas?"

"Yeah, man."

"Make that motherfucker hurt, will ya?" I plead.

"Count on it," he responds. We bump each other's fist in unification.

"Let's get this done," Axe grinds out.

Atticus and his men take the back of the house as we follow Silas' lead at the front. He holds up his hand and counts us down, one finger, two fingers then on the third one, he lifts his foot up and slams it on the door. It swings open and we rush inside. The sight that greets us has me holding back the vomit that wants to spew from me. "That's just fucking gross," I spit. My father has Daria face planted into the cushion of the couch as he drills into her from behind.

"Fucking nasty cunt!" Axe hollers as he grabs the sleeve of my shirt and drags me behind him. I hear the two disgusting individuals screaming in the front room as the men place them into custody. It's a good thing Law and Chief stayed behind, I doubt they'd be able to sit back and allow the Nelsons to take in the dumb-witted imbeciles in good conscience.

When Axe and I make it to the last room on the left, I rush

ahead of him. Making my way over to the cheaply made crib, I look down and see my baby girl sleeping peacefully. At least Daria has somewhat taken care of her. She seems to have on a fresh diaper and I notice the empty bottle sitting next to the older than dirt rocking chair. Picking her up, I swaddle her to my chest and sigh in relief. "Come on, Maxum, let's get her out of this filth," Axe says in distaste.

"Couldn't agree more, Grandpa," I reply, earning me a glare from my president, brother, and future father-in-law.

"I refuse to be called Grandpa, Son. We'll have to come up with a better name and train her to use it."

"She's not a dog," I protest.

"Maybe not, but if Lucy can learn to use a damn elevator, then Violet can learn to call me something more suave than Grandpa." I chuckle at his words as we walk through the back of the house to the back door. I do not want to see those two naked and on display. Also, I don't want those fuckers to place another eye on my girl. They've seen the last of her that they ever will.

Lily

Mom drove us all to the hospital in her SUV. She has the biggest vehicle, the only one that we could all fit comfortably in. As soon as the car is in park, I rush out, not waiting on the others to catch up. "Don't fall, Lily!" Mom calls out. I wave her off over my shoulder, not once slowing down. I have one mission in mind, that's to hold my baby and kiss my old man.

As I make my way through the maze of hallways, I finally hear my dad's voice and follow it. They're in the waiting room, and Dad is pissed off. "This baby was *kidnapped* from this hospital! She should be a priority," he roars at the pale faced receptionist. "I'm gonna start fucking things up if a doctor doesn't look her over!"

"Sir." A wanna be cop comes up to my dad and says, "I'm gonna have to ask you to calm down."

"You are not seriously saying this to him," I growl from behind them, causing them all to twirl around, eyes wide at the vehemence coming out of me.

"Lil," Maxum says with relief. I run to him and wrap my arms around him and our daughter. After a few seconds, I take my daughter from Maxum and pull her to me. I check her over as best as I can. I count her toes, just like I did after she was born, smell her sweet baby scent and am able to relax for the first time since she was taken from us.

Mom walks up and says, "I just called Dr. Sandoval. She's calling into the ER but is headed here now to check Violet over and get her readmitted." I feel the tension ease slightly at her words, even though Maxum sneers at the security officer and Dad glares at the receptionist.

"We are *all* staying here until she's discharged," Dad states, looking at Maxum. I find it funny that he's pointing at the floor as he says this. He's not playing around, and I'm eternally grateful for that.

"Absofuckinglutely," my old man replies. "We're not going anywhere and they better get used to that fact."

I see some stuffy looking suit coming toward us. He stops in front of me and Maxum and says, "I'm Dexter Holloway, the hospital administrator. I understand we had a situation occur and want to assure you that we will do everything to ensure it doesn't happen again."

"A situation?" Dad hisses out. "You're calling my granddaughter's kidnapping a *situation*? What kind of two-bit, inept place are you running here? Are you aware that the so-called nurse who was often in charge of her care had false credentials? No, I don't think you understand what's going to happen from here on out. First, we're going to own this fucking hospital. I've already got Elijah Jackson working on the paperwork on behalf of my daughter and son-in-law. Second, we will be staying, all of us, while

Violet is under your so-called care, so you need to put us in one of those suites and make sure there are sufficient cots for the women at least. You hear me?"

"Braxton," Mom says, trying to calm him.

"No, Cara. This piece of shit allowed this to happen because of his shoddy hiring practices. He's partially responsible for what happened to Violet, as well as the terror that our daughter and her old man have been going through." I see when Mom gets it because she turns on the man.

"He's right. If I were you, I'd go back to your fancy office and start calling your legal department because I believe when the dust finally settles, my daughter is going to own this place." With Aunt DJ and Uncle Hatch glowering at him, Mr. Holloway slowly backs away and heads to the elevators.

"Lily?" I turn when I hear Dr. Sandoval's voice. She's rushing toward us and it's obvious that she was relaxing at home because she's not wearing her normal scrubs and white coat. No, she has a pair of character leggings and a long, oversized t-shirt on. She reaches us and gently takes Violet from my arms before she motions for us to follow her. "Let's get this little miss checked out, shall we?"

WE'RE NOW ENSCONCED IN THE LARGEST SUITE THEY HAVE on the maternity ward. Violet has a new identity bracelet, and each one of my family is sporting the adult version. Dr. Sandoval made the decision to bring the incubator into the room versus taking Violet to the nursery, so we're sitting around and watching my little girl as she soaks up the light. "Those are kind of cute," Rae admits, pointing to her blinders. "Kind of looks like a sleep mask, doesn't it?"

I giggle because I had thought that the first time I saw her under the lamp. "It's too bad they're plain. They could get the decorated ones at least so the babies look cute," I reply.

"Lily?" Maxum asks as he comes up to where I'm standing. "You got a minute?"

Maxum

I'M NERVOUS AS FUCK RIGHT NOW, BUT WHAT BETTER TIME and place to ask my old lady to marry me than in front of her family. Axe had Nan go to his house and grab the ring and he gave it to me when we were on the way to the hospital. I figure this might help us all to put this behind us. She looks at me with her brow raised, so I lean in and quickly kiss her. Nothing major, of course, not with her dad and brother in the room at least.

"What's wrong, Maxum?" she inquires.

I don't think, I just drop to one knee and grab her hand. "Lily Callahan, you've captivated me for a very long time, even when I thought there was no hope you'd be interested. You're my best friend, my lover, my old lady, and the momma to our beautiful little girl, but there's one thing more that I need. You to be my wife. Will you marry me, Lily? Keep being the sunshine to my darkness? Give me a houseful of kids?"

I watch as tears form in her eyes and silently slip down her cheeks, my heart in my throat. "Yes, yes, yes, to all of it!" she whisper-yells so she doesn't wake Violet up. "I love you, Maxum, so damn much, and I want to do life with you by my side."

I slip the ring on her finger and stand, pulling her into my arms. This time, I don't give a flying fuck who is standing around, I claim her lips in a kiss designed to show her everything I'm feeling. "Get a room!" Tig hollers. Without raising my head, I flip him off and can hear the laughter ringing throughout the room.

23

LILY

It's been a couple of weeks since Violet returned to us. She was discharged three days after being brought back into the hospital. Maxum has a surprise for me, he won't tell me what it is, he simply stated that Violet and I needed to be ready to go. That was twenty minutes ago and he only gave me half an hour to prepare.

"Alright, Violet, we have you changed, your bag ready to go, now all we need is your daddy to get here and pick us up." Last week, Maxum brought home a Chevrolet Tahoe for me to drive, insisting that we needed the room for our growing family. I asked him how many kids he thought we'd be having to fill such a large vehicle. He simply smiled and told me as many as we produced. I hope he's not planning on knocking me up every year until we can form our own football team. That's ludicrous, and my uterus will protest profusely.

"Honey, I'm home!" I hear called out as I pick up Violet.

"I'm in Violet's room, give me a sec," I call back. "Okay, baby girl, let's go see what Dad has up his sleeve." She opens her eyes briefly as if to say, 'let's do this' then conks back out. Way to have your mom's back, Violet.

Walking into the front room, I see Maxum nervously pacing. "Y'all ready?" he questions with nervousness radiating from him.

"You're freaking me out, Maxum." I watch him as he turns and looks over at the two of us.

"I'm freaking out that you won't like what I've done," he states.

"What *have* you done?" I would place my hands on my

hips in a show of domination, but I've got Violet bundled up next to me.

"Umm… it's better if I show you than tell you." He bites his lip. "Here, let me take her from you."

"Maxum Bass, if you think holding our daughter will save you from my wrath, you have another thing coming, mister."

"I would never use our daughter as a shield," he claims. I can see the mischief dancing behind his eyes.

"You're lying out your damn teeth, Maxum."

"Am not," he says, all but pulling Violet away from me and placing her on his chest. "I look good carrying a baby, huh?"

"Stop," I giggle, having a hard time staying upset with him when he does things like this. "But yeah, you look good holding our daughter."

"Come on, baby. We need to get going." He grabs Violet's carrier and bag.

"Alright, you do all the heavy lifting and I'll sit back and enjoy the view." I waggle my eyebrows at my admission. He chuckles causing Violet to stir. "Shh… I want her to sleep the whole way."

"When does our girl not sleep in the car?" he asks. This is true, she loves the car and sleeps peacefully every time we drive somewhere. It's my magic baby sleep machine.

Maxum

I'M NOT ONE-HUNDRED PERCENT SURE THAT SHE'LL BE happy I did this without her, but I know she's going to fall in love with our home. "Close your eyes," I order as we come close to the street I need to turn on.

"Really?" she questions, but complies.

"Yes, really."

"Fine, Maxum. How long do I have to keep them closed for? I get car sick when I try to sleep. I don't want to upchuck in my new Tahoe."

"It won't be long, I swear," I state as I turn down the road leading to our place. As I finally reach our driveway, I admire the work that Jaxson did to the exterior of the house, as well as the crew he found who updated the landscaping. Pulling to a stop in front of the house, I say, "You can open your eyes, baby."

I watch her closely as she opens her eyes and see her gasp. "Why are we at the Heyward place?" she asks.

"Because it's now the Bass House," I reply. I see when she realizes what I've said because her eyes grow wide and she practically jumps in her seat. "You want to see our new home, Lil?" I ask.

"Uh, not to sound like a kid but duh, Maxum. I've always loved this place; how did you know?"

"Because every time we drove by, you'd say you wished it would go on the market. Now, you stay put, I'm getting you out then I'll get the baby." I chuckle as I hear her seat-belt unclick and know she's doing all she can to keep from rushing up the steps of the wraparound porch. As I open her door, she launches herself into my arms and starts kissing me.

"I love it already, Maxum, just because you remembered something so small," she says between kisses. "Now, grab our daughter and give me the tour," she demands.

When we both get to the top of the steps, I set the carrier down and unlock the door. "Hold on, baby, gonna do this shit right," I murmur, before I scoop her up and carry her across the threshold. Once she regains her feet, I turn and pick Violet's carrier up then snag Lily's hand in mine. "Let's do the tour, baby."

Lily

I'm blown away with the attention to detail that Maxum put into the renovations and upgrades. Years ago, when this house was on the Christmas lights tour, I saw the inside and fell in love with the high ceilings and openness of the rooms. I vowed then that if it ever went on the market, I wanted it as my very own and he made that dream come true.

He's made all my dreams come true.

"Maxum, the bed is huge," I whisper, looking around the master bedroom. He showed me the rest of the house, but saved 'our room' for last.

"Jaxson decided we should have a custom-sized bed," he states. When I glance at him, he waggles his eyebrows at me and I feel myself reacting.

"Oh, really?" I tease, swaying my hips as I walk closer to him and place my hand on his chest.

"You minx, we've still got a few weeks to wait," he replies. I can see his erection through his jeans and a thrill runs through me that despite still being a bit chunky from the baby weight, he doesn't care.

"I can't wait, Maxum," I whisper. "It's been too long."

"Tell me about it, baby," he grits out as I press myself closer.

"Why do we have to wait again? Can't we start christening our new house?" I ask.

He takes a deep shuddering breath before saying, "Because you need to get cleared by Dr. Sandoval and make sure everything's back where it should be or some shit. How the hell should I know why they make us wait? I just know that's what the doctor said and so do the books, so as hard as it is, we're waiting." He uses that growly voice I love so much and I want to do nothing more than sink to my knees and take matters into my own hands and mouth. Hmm, something to think about for later!

"If you say so," I reply, sticking out my lower lip and pouting.

"Baby, I'd like nothing more than to bend you over the end of the bed and pound into you until we wake up Violet, but I refuse to do anything that could hurt you so I won't. But I will kiss you."

"Fine," I grumble. He growls at me and before I know

what's happening, he's kissing me breathless. "I know we can't make love, but maybe we can find something else that'll ease some of the tension, biker boy," I whisper when we finally pull apart.

"What did you have in mind?" he asks, a grin forming on his handsome face.

I feel my face heating and look over his shoulder as I say, "I can always go down on you."

He tilts my chin up and replies, "I think we need to go make that happen for both of us, baby." Then he kisses me again until I'm panting and my panties feel like they're soaked.

"Take me home, Maxum. I want our first time in our new home to be when we can make love, not just fool around like teenagers," I state.

"Anything you want, sweetheart." He picks up Violet's carrier and takes my hand in his. "I'm glad you like the house, Lil. I was so fucking scared you'd get mad at me for doing this without you."

"I love how you take care of me, of both of us," I reply, nodding at Violet. "Even when we were apart, you were still trying to take care of me by seeing Dr. Graves. I'm so glad you found her because she's been a huge help to both of us."

And she truly has been because I nearly lost my mind when I found out who had taken Violet. Maxum held me while he told me that my birth mother, the person who dumped me with Aunt Paisley as a baby, lied about her credentials and then stole Violet. When he advised me that his father was seeing Daria and was at the house where they had taken Violet, I lost my shit. I went for my gun, intent on finding where the Nelson brothers had taken them so I could look them both in the eye and put a bullet between each of their eyes. Or maybe multiple bullets, seeing as I had two extra clips ready to go. Maxum called Dr. Graves and she got us in that same day, Violet tucked between us. She helped me come to terms with the fact that I would not likely know what happened, but the reality was that the Nelson brothers would take care of it and it was over.

My nightmares stopped that night. Oh, it's not always smooth sailing as we adjust to living with each other. I love sleeping with a fan on and Maxum doesn't. I smile when I remember how he came home with a small fan for my nightstand on the same day I brought him an electric blanket for his side.

"What has you smiling, Lil?" he asks as we make our way home.

"I was thinking about how much Dr. Graves helped after,

you know. And how we're learning to compromise since we started living together."

"Baby, I love you. If we have to compromise so that we keep growing as a couple, so be it. It's our relationship, no one else's, and I'll do whatever it takes to keep it growing stronger." His words bring tears to my eyes and I reach over to take his hand in mine, the diamond of my engagement ring sparkling.

"Have I ever told you how much it means that you gave me Nan's ring? I remember when I was a little girl, I would pretend with it and one day, when I was about ten, she told me that someday, it would be mine when the right man came along and asked my dad for permission to marry me."

EPILOGUE

Lily

Today is the day. I become Mrs. Maxum Bass in a little less than thirty minutes. I've been primped and pampered at the salon. My hair is styled to perfection, my nails are freshly manicured and I had a relaxing pedicure. I'm wearing a short-skirted wedding dress, not white because I would have it dirty in no time, but it's a soft baby blue color. I'm wearing my new cut over it proclaiming I'm the property of Maxum. It finally came in two days ago and I haven't had the heart to take it off since he gave it to me at my ceremony.

"Lily! Stop daydreaming and let me put the final touches on your makeup," Mom demands as she sighs, but gives me a small smile in return.

"Sorry, Mom. I can't stop thinking about all the good things that have happened in my life."

"I remember those days well," she grins in response.

"Will it ever get old?" I ask her.

"Will what ever get old?" she asks back.

"This feeling. Like when Maxum walks through the front door, my heart beats so fast I fear it'll jump from my chest. When he smiles, I can't help but smile back."

"Being able to finish each other's sentences?" I laugh when she says this. "It'll never get old, Lily, but it will always feel like the first time you ever saw him. You'll never go a day without loving him, admiring him and wishing you could stay in his arms twenty-four seven."

"Good to know," I respond.

"Girls! Stop gallivanting around, would ya?" Nan interjects, popping her hip and giving us a look of dismay. "That man downstairs is driving everyone mad. If you're ready to do this, we can start early," she huffs.

"I'm ready!"

"She's ready," Mom and I both blurt out at the same exact time.

As I stand in the back out of sight, I watch as my sister Layne pulls Violet down the aisle in a little red wagon. It's decorated with lace and has the same color bows as my dress on each side. She's in her carrier, and Layne is tossing flowers out as she pulls her down the aisle. Since we don't have a ring bearer, we've placed the pillow on Violet's lap. She'll be both because Landon proclaimed he was too damn old to play the part.

"You ready to do this? If not, if you've changed your mind, I can have one of the guys get a getaway car for us and we won't turn back. As soon as I grab your mom and Violet anyway," Dad says, and I can see how serious he is about this.

"Dad, I'm sure. He's the love of my life and I can't wait to spend the rest of my days growing old with him."

"I suppose we should get going then. This song is our cue, but make sure you're positive before we take that first step," he continues.

"Dad!"

"Alright!" he pouts. "But Layne is going to be thirty before she does this to me."

"Watch what you say, Dad. Don't want to make any bets and watch you eat those words."

"Not funny, young lady."

"I think I'm rather brilliant, personally," I say as we begin walking down the aisle to the wedding march. Today is absolutely perfect!

Maxum

WATCHING LILY WALK TOWARD ME, I FEEL A LUMP GATHER in my throat and my heart starts pounding. "You can always back out, brother," Jaxson leans in and whispers. "Me and Talon will hold off Luca and Axe while you make your getaway."

"Shut it, fucker," I growl, low enough that only he can hear me. "She's my forever and I'm not ever giving that up."

"Good answer. Got your back, though, brother. Just wanted you to know."

As Axe reaches us, he waits for instructions from Luca, who got ordained so he could perform our wedding since he wanted to be a part of our day. Axe kisses Lily's cheek, gives me a warning glare, then moves to sit with Cara, who now has our baby in the cradle of her arms. I lose myself in the words he's saying, mentally vowing each and every promise he speaks to the woman at my side. "Maxum, you had something you wanted to say," Luca prompts. I nod and turn slightly so we're now facing one another.

"Lily, we met so many years ago that there's not a happy time in my life that doesn't have you in the memory. When it became obvious that we shared a mutual attraction, I fought it with everything I had because I truly didn't feel I deserved someone like you, or the family that came along with you. Only, you showed me differently. Through our darkest days and our brightest nights, you've been the one constant, the reason I get up every day. Adding Violet to our lives has only enriched it further. I look forward to all of our tomorrows, the good and the bad, the happy and the sad, as long as you're by my side. I love you, my Lily. Now and forever."

I can hear the sniffles coming from the old ladies, but my focus is on her. I see one tear slip out and slide down her cheek and reach out to catch it on my finger. "I'll always catch your tears, sweetheart," I murmur.

"Lily, it's your turn," Luca instructs.

She looks up at me, her smile a bit wobbly as she tries to control her emotions. "Maxum, I've known since the first time I saw you that you were the one for me. I know it took us a few years to get to that point, but my faith in us never wavered, even when you pushed me away in the mistaken belief that you didn't deserve me… deserve us. Violet is a blessing in so many ways and while in some ways, we did things backwards, I wouldn't change a minute of any of it, as long as the end result was us, standing here in front of family and loved ones, proclaiming our love for one another, and saying our vows. I loved you yesterday, I love you today, and I'll love you tomorrow until I draw my last breath."

Luca has us exchange our rings and I hear her gasp as I slide the wedding band on her finger. I had it specially designed to include an infinity symbol with diamonds and on each side, our birthstones. "With the exchange of the rings, it's my privilege to announce that in accordance with the great State of Texas, I now pronounce you man and wife. You may kiss your bride."

I draw her into my arms and cup her face. Looking into her eyes, I whisper so only she can hear, "I love you, Lily," before I kiss her, uncaring of the eyes watching.

As I finally go to pull away, I hear Tig yell, "Get a room!"

The End

WANNA KNOW WHAT HAPPENS WITH DARIA AND KILLIAN? This will be answered in book 3 of the Nelson Brothers… Seeking Our Destiny, coming January 2020.

God blesses the broken roads in our lives in so many ways. We hope you enjoyed the journey with Maxum and Lily. Next up in the kids is Restoring Tig, in the New Beginnings series.

Tig is a character we can't wait to write.

Will he and Danika make it through his issues, or will it be too late once he comes to grips with his past? Stay tuned, these questions and more will be answered.

LIBERTY PARKER'S FOLLOW LINKS:

Liberty Parker

Where fantasy, romance and dreams collide.

Website:

http://authorlibertyparker.com

Goodreads:

https://www.goodreads.com/author/show/14035441.Liberty_Parker

BookBub:

https://www.bookbub.com/authors/liberty-parker

Newsletter sign up form:

https://landing.mailerlite.com/webforms/landing/s1v0k0

Facebook Author Page:

https://www.facebook.com/authorlibertyparker/

Liberty's Luscious Ladies:

https://www.facebook.com/groups/1153797384736487/

Rebel Guardians Insiders:

https://www.facebook.com/groups/280929722515781/

Twisted Iron Groupies:

https://www.facebook.com/groups/2088172217913867/

Twitter:

https://twitter.com/authorlparker

Instagram:

https://www.instagram.com/libertyauthor/

Book order form:

https://goo.gl/forms/47PjnbSrSBj5hY5R2

DARLENE TALLMAN'S FOLLOW LINKS:

Facebook Author Page:

https://www.facebook.com/darlenetallmanauthor/

Darlene's Dolls Group Page:

https://www.facebook.com/groups/1024089434417791/

Rebel Guardians Insiders:

https://www.facebook.com/groups/280929722515781/

Newsletter Subscriber Link:

http://eepurl.com/dEaxGj

Goodreads:

https://www.goodreads.com/author/show/
15709175.Darlene_Tallman

Bookbub:

https://www.bookbub.com/authors/darlene-tallman

ALSO BY LIBERTY PARKER

Rage Ryders MC

1. Taken By Lies

2. Taken By Rage

2.5. Taken By Vegas

3. Taken By Sadistic

4. Taken By Chaos

5. Taken By Temptation

Rage Ryders Templeton

Faithfully Devoted

Diva's Ink

1. Blank Canvas

Audible

2. Clean Slate

3. Beautiful Template

Dreamcatchers MC

1. Charlee's Choices

2. Capturing Dreams

Surrogacy

1. What Should've Been

Crossroad Soldiers MC

1. Walking The Crossroad

2. Our Cross To Bear

Rebel Guardians MC (with Darlene Tallman)

Braxton

Hatchet

Chief

Smokey & Bandit

Law

Capone

A Twisted Kind Of Love

Rebel Guardians Next Generation (with Darlene Tallman)

1. Talon & Claree

2. Jaxson & Ralynn

New Beginnings (with Darlene Tallman)

1. Reclaiming Maysen

2. Reviving Luca

Nelson Brothers (with Darlene Tallman)

1. Seeking Our Revenge

2. Seeking Our Forever

Twisted Iron MC (with Kayce Kyle)

1. Mercenary And His Outlaw

2. Fueling The Edg

3. Sandman's Awakening

Old Ladies Club (with Kayce Kyle, Erin Osborne and Darlene Tallman)

1. Old Ladies Club - Wild Kings MC

2. The Old Ladies Club - Soul Shifterz MC

3. Old Ladies Club - Rebel Guardians MC

4. Old Ladies Club - Rage Ryders MC

ALSO BY DARLENE TALLMAN

Bountiful Harvest

His Firefly

His Christmas Pixie

Her Kinsman-Redeemer

Operation Valentine

His Forever

Forgiveness

Christmas With Dixie

Our Last First Kiss

Draegon: The Falder Clan - Book One

Scars of the Soul

Hale's Song

The Mischief Kitties (with Cherry Shephard)

The Mischief Kitties in Bampires & Ghosts & New Friends, Oh My!

The Mischief Kitties in the Great Glitter Caper

The Mischief Kitties in You Can't Takes Our Chicken

The Black Tuxedos MC

1. The Black Tuxedos MC - Reese

2. Nick - The Black Tuxedos MC

Rebel Guardians MC (with Liberty Parker)

Braxton

Hatchet

Chief

Smokey & Bandit

Law

Capone

A Twisted Kind Of Love

Rebel Guardians Next Generation (with Liberty Parker)

1. Talon & Claree

2. Jaxson & Ralynn

New Beginnings (with Liberty Parker)

1. Reclaiming Maysen

2. Reviving Luca

Nelson Brothers (with Liberty Parker)

1. Seeking Our Revenge

2. Seeking Our Forever

Old Ladies Club (with Kayce Kyle, Erin Osborne and Liberty Parker)

1. Old Ladies Club - Wild Kings MC

2. The Old Ladies Club - Soul Shifterz MC

3. Old Ladies Club - Rebel Guardians MC

4. Old Ladies Club - Rage Ryders MC

With Various Other Authors

Poetry: Dreams You Catch

Made in the USA
Middletown, DE
08 March 2020

85885716R00156